Undying Resilience

Ruthless Desires 3

Elira Firethorn

To the adults from my childhood
who supported my writing.
I'll never forget you.

Playlist &
Storyboard

Playlist:

Rescue My Heart – Liz Longley

Beautiful Undone – Laura Doggett

Waiting Game – BANKS

Alone In A Room – Asking Alexandria

Sick Thoughts – Lewis Blissett

The Wall – PatrickReza

Hurts So Good – Maximillian & Kina Version – Astrid S

Into Your Arms (feat. Ava Max) – Witt Lowry

Be Together – Major Lazer, Wild Belle

Dirty Mind – Boy Epic

Tonight – R3YAN, BLVKES

vicious – Tate McRae

Storyboard:

You can find Undying Resilience's storyboard by going to
pinterest.com/elirafirethorn.

Before You Read

Undying Resilience is a dark romance book intended for people over the age of eighteen. Please read over this list to make sure there's nothing inside this book that could affect you negatively. Put your mental health first please!

Emotional: The mention and aftereffects of emotional/verbal abuse during childhood (flashbacks, aversion to vulnerability, touch, and opening up emotionally), blurred lines of good and evil, a corruption arc of one of the main characters, depression, running anxious thoughts, nightmares, and a fear of water.

Physical: The mention of domestic violence (murder of multiple romantic partners [off-page]), a mention of a child dying (off-page), murder, kidnapping, forced starvation and dehydration, violence, multiple full scenes of torture by nonfatal drowning, a fade to black torture and murder scene that includes knives and cutting, and a torture and murder scene that includes fatal drowning.

Sexual: This book also contains explicit sex scenes that include bondage, edging, impact play, spit play, domination and submission, and degradation. Everything is consensual.

Undying Resilience ends on a happy-for-now mild cliffhanger with an implication for what will happen in the next book.

As is the case with all the books in this series, you won't find many physical descriptions of the main characters so you can imagine them however you'd like. You will, however, find the occasional description of a side character here and there.

The scenes in this book aren't meant to be a guide to BDSM or kink. This is a work of *fiction* and should be read as such.

undying RESILIENCE

CHAPTER ONE

Wren

Note: This book is much darker than the first two in the series. Please flip back and read the Before You Read section if you haven't already.

"Harder."

"I don't know if I can," I pant.

"You can, and you will. *Harder*, Wren."

I steady myself. Then I pull one of the first jab-punch combinations Rhett taught me. I throw as much force as I possibly can into the punching bag.

"Better," Rhett says. Then he hands me my water bottle. "Drink up."

Grabbing it with gloves on is awkward as hell, but I manage. Thankfully Rhett had the sense to pop the lid open for me.

We're in the home gym at the guys' mansion. It's been over a week since I was dragged into the Williams job, and from what I can tell, all three guys are pretty worried they exposed me to their world so quickly.

Rhett seems the most agitated. After what happened last Tuesday, he's been adamant about me learning how to protect myself. We had our first training session earlier this week, and now we're back at it again today.

I took a series of self-defense classes in college, but I'm pretty rusty on most of the moves I learned. Still, the knowledge is helping me grasp what Rhett throws at me without too much trouble.

"How did you guys learn all of this?" I ask after taking a couple sips of water.

"Learn what? How to throw a punch?" There's a hint of amusement in his tone.

"I guess, yeah." There's a lot I'm curious about, like how they got into their profession in the first place. But this is a start.

"I started taking martial arts classes when I was young for . . . reasons." A shadow crosses over Rhett's face, and he looks past me, almost like he's staring directly into his childhood. "Ell and O joined me later on."

His unspoken words hang in the air between us. *After Sammy was killed.*

"Everything else followed," Rhett continues, almost like he can sense that I want to know more. "As we kept looking more and more into who killed Sammy, we made a decent amount of connections. Sometimes we had to do favors for people in exchange for information. It taught us a lot, and it all led us to where we are now."

"Which is where, exactly?"

"Not close enough." His voice is clipped as he takes my water bottle, nodding to the punching bag. "Go again."

"Close enough to what?" *To killing Ludo?*

"Enough talking, Wren. You need to focus."

I'm not sure what exactly caused Rhett's mood to sour, other than the mention of Sammy. I have no desire to make it worse, so I turn back to the punching bag.

For the next twenty minutes, Rhett coaches me on my form, teaching me a new combination when he thinks I'm ready. As time passes, he seems to cool off. Or maybe he's just hiding whatever's going on in his head better.

After a while, he has me take my gloves off. Then he leads me to a large black mat on the floor. I stop at the edge, watching him. On Monday, he started teaching me some self-defense moves. They're helpful, but they usually require me hitting or kicking him in some sort of way.

When Rhett sees the uneasiness on my face, he says, "Why does this part make you uncomfortable?"

"I'm afraid I'll hurt you." I look down. I know it's stupid—I should be more worried about Rhett hurting me than the other way around. But the last thing I want to do is cause him more pain.

Rhett lets out a half-laugh. "You really think I'd let you inflict that much damage on me, sweetheart?"

"I . . ."

"Come here."

Grudgingly, I step onto the mat.

He grabs my hand and pulls me toward him. "I can handle a couple punches and kicks, Wren. But you know what I *won't* be able to handle?"

"What?"

"Someone hurting you. And if I have to deal with a little pain to make sure you know how to adequately keep yourself safe, then so be it."

"But I don't—"

"*Wren.*"

I sigh. "Okay."

He lets my hand go with a little squeeze. "Fists up."

We spar for a while. There's a lot of stopping and starting as he corrects my form and gives me tips to help me remember things. Then after a while we switch to takedowns. Well, *one* takedown, because it's really damn hard to grasp.

"Like . . . like this?" I say on the fifth try.

Rhett chuckles. And then he somehow flips me around and throws me onto my back with absolutely no effort. "No. Not like that. You leave yourself open to some pretty nasty attacks."

"How . . . ugh," I groan. Then I laugh, rolling my eyes. "And I thought I had you for a second."

Rhett gets onto his hands and knees and crawls over me, not bothering to affirm what I said. He presses a chaste kiss to my lips as a barely-there smile flickers across his features.

I let out a huff. "You only *let* me think I was gonna do it, didn't you?"

He shrugs. "Was just waiting to see what you'd do. Doesn't change the fact that you're doing better than the other day."

"Hmmph." I cross my arms, trying to glare up at him, but it turns into a grin pretty fast.

With another kiss, he says, "You're going to need to be more vigilant now, Wren. I'm teaching you how to fight in case you ever find yourself caught off guard. But the key here is to *not* let that happen."

I nod. "Should I start carrying a weapon or something?"

He frowns. "Like what?"

"A knife?"

"God no. Absolutely not. You don't know how to fight with one. And until you do, you're more likely to end up with it stuck in *your* body than your opponent's."

Grimacing, I say, "Oh."

"We'll be here to watch your back, sweetheart. And when we're not, we have friends who will help look out for you."

My stomach sinks. "You're talking about tomorrow."

He nods. "You can still come with us if you've changed your mind."

I shake my head.

Tomorrow—Friday—the guys are leaving town for a job. They haven't told me where exactly they're going, just that it's still within the States. When they told me I could come, all I could think of was how close Tyler got to me and Oliver when we were in the hunter's stand. It still sends a shiver through me even now.

"We'd keep you safe," Rhett says. "You wouldn't come with us for the kill—you'd stay at the cabin we'll be spending a couple nights at. No one would even know where you are."

Staying silent, I run my hands over his chest. There's something comforting about him hovering over me like this. It's a similar feeling to being close to the guys in general. They brought a sense of safety into my life that I haven't had in a long time.

Still, I'm not ready to go with them on another job—even if I won't be with them during the times they're actually working. I can't help but worry that somehow I *will* end up with them, just like with the Williams job. And that's not something I can handle again. Not right now, at least.

"I don't want to be away from the three of you," I say eventually. "But going with you scares me. Because of last time."

Rhett nods. "I understand."

I press my lips together. I can tell that he doesn't like the idea of leaving me behind. I don't like it either, but staying home sounds safer, even if it means being alone.

"We'll make sure you're protected," he says. "Finn will ensure you get to work and back home safe. And anywhere else you need to go."

"Okay," I whisper. "Thank you."

"We'd do anything to keep you safe, sweetheart." Again, Rhett leans down, capturing my mouth with his. This kiss is far from chaste, but it's not sexual or hungry either. It's more of a silent reassurance, like he doesn't know how else to affirm what he said.

My hands move from Rhett's chest to his shoulders. I pull him down so his body is pressed against mine, wrapping my arms around his neck. And just like that, our kiss turns heated.

Rhett groans. "We should keep training." But as he says it, he snakes his arms around my body and rolls us so he's on his back and I'm lying on top of him.

"We should," I say, my voice completely lacking conviction. I adjust myself so I'm sitting up, straddling Rhett. Slowly, I roll my hips into his, smiling at how hard he is.

He smirks. "But I'm not one to pass up an opportunity to have you all to myself."

"I was hoping you'd say that." I give him a mischievous grin. My fingers travel down his chest to his sides, where I tickle him lightly.

Rhett grunts, grabbing my wrists. "You really want to start something you can't win, Wren?"

Twisting my arms from his grasp, I move for his armpits. But before I'm even halfway there, he starts tickling my stomach. With a squeal, I try to pull his hands away from my body, but he's too strong.

"I'll ask you again, sweetheart. Do you really want to start this?" His eyes are darkened with an unspoken challenge: *Keep going, and I'll make you pay.*

I pause. "What happens if I say yes?"

"Same as last time. Except it won't be your pretty little ass that gets spanked. And don't think I won't tickle you until you can't breathe. Because I will."

With a delighted gasp, I look down at him, gauging the emotions on his face. I'm pretty sure he wants this, but I don't want to make him feel like he has to do something if he doesn't want to. They've been so good about making sure I'm always comfortable, and I want to do the same for them.

"Do you like giving out punishments?" I ask.

"Only certain ones. And only with the right people."

I hesitate. "Is this . . ."

He nods. "This is fine. I'll tell you if it's not."

"So I can tickle you?" I whisper.

He chuckles. "You can *try*."

And with that, he flips me onto my back. I laugh, tickling his sides again. But it only takes him a few seconds before he has both of my wrists in a tight hold with one hand. With the other, he yanks my shirt up, lightly brushing his fingers over the sensitive skin of my stomach.

I squirm, trying to free my hands, but it's no use. Rhett tickles me until I'm a panting, giggling mess. When he finally lets me go, I gasp in a breath, grinning up at him.

"Kiss me," I say.

He lowers himself, propping himself on his elbows. For a split second, he stares down at me, his gaze traveling over my face. Something passes over his features. Discomfort? Worry? Unease? Maybe all three?

"I love your smile," he murmurs.

He kisses me before I can respond. I'm so thrown off by the compliment—and the wave of emotions he obviously felt before saying the words—that it takes me a second to remember why I asked him to kiss me.

I've got him now.

Moaning into Rhett's mouth, I flatten my palms against his sides. Slowly, I move my hands down his body until my fingers find the sensitive skin by his hipbones.

"Shit," he grunts, his body jerking away from my touch. "You sneaky little devil."

I giggle, tickling him again before he grabs my hands.

"I was thinking of letting you off easy," he says. "Not anymore."

Standing, Rhett pulls me with him. Once I'm steady on my feet, he lets me go, crossing his arms and giving me a chilling look.

"Clothes. Off."

I scramble to obey his command, throwing everything onto the mat.

He steps toward me until we're so close we're almost touching. "So eager to be punished," he muses, tilting my chin up with a single finger.

I whimper, staring into his eyes. The first thing I ever noticed about Rhett was how strong his gaze was—like he could see right into my mind with a simple glance. I still feel the same way now.

Keeping his gaze locked with mine, Rhett nods to a piece of workout equipment. I saw Elliot doing bench presses on it the other day.

"Lie on your back," Rhett says, pushing me toward the bench. "That's it. Now spread your legs for me."

Doing so makes me feel overexposed, but I still obey, holding my legs steady with my hands. Rhett smirks, taking me in, and I can't help but let out an impatient whine. I want him touching me, even if it's his hand spanking my clit until I scream.

"Take a deep breath," he says, stroking one of my calves.

I inhale, my eyes falling shut. And just as I start to exhale, I feel the sharp sting of Rhett's palm slapping against my clit. My eyes fly open as I yelp, all tension returning to my body. Instinctively, I start to close my legs, but the scolding look Rhett gives me has me opening them again.

He *tsks*. "Such a bad slut. Do you really want to make this harder on yourself?"

I whimper, shaking my head.

"Then keep your legs open and your eyes on me." He smacks my clit again, and this time I let out a half-moan, half-scream. Before I can recover, he delivers another blow. "Can't let you enjoy it too much."

"Holy shit," I pant.

"I'd ask if you've learned your lesson, but I think I know the answer."

I can't help but grin.

Rhett smacks my clit one more time. It stings, but it feels good, too. With another smirk, he circles my entrance with a single finger before holding it up to the light. "Look how wet you are from taking your punishment. Such a naughty girl."

"More," I moan.

"More pain? Or more pleasure?"

"Both," I whisper.

He brings his palm against my clit again, and I arch my back with a scream. Then he uses a finger to gently stroke my clit, his gaze still locked with mine.

"You want to come, sweetheart?"

I nod.

"You're going to have to work for it."

"Anything," I pant.

He sheds his clothes before pulling me off the bench. It only takes us a second to settle with him lying on his back on the mat and me straddling him. I slide down onto his cock with a moan.

"Fuck," Rhett groans, thrusting up into me. He does it again, and again.

I grin. "I thought I was going to work for it."

With an annoyed smirk, he smacks my ass. "Then get moving."

I start off slowly, letting myself adjust. As I pick up my pace, I lean forward and place my hands on his chest for balance.

"Fuck, just like that, sweetheart." Rhett grabs my shoulders. "Touch yourself for me. I'll make sure you don't fall."

My clit is sensitive, so I stroke it gently, adding just the right amount of friction. Just as I'm finding a good rhythm, I hear the garage door opening. Elliot and Oliver must be home.

"Just in time," Rhett says. He starts pumping his hips to match my movements. It makes everything feel ten times better, and he must be able to tell, because he grins. "Are you going to come for them, Wren?"

"Yes, fuck—yes. Rhett. Rhett, I'm so close."

"Not yet," he says tightly. "I know you want them to hear."

I groan. He's right, but I can't take this for much longer.

The door leading to the garage opens and closes, which means Elliot and Oliver are in the small hallway that leads to here and the kitchen.

"Rhett," I sob. I can't help it. My orgasm is barreling toward me, and unless he slows down, I'm not going to be able to hold back.

"Scream for them, sweetheart."

I do—not because he told me to, but because I can't help myself when he finally lets me come. My orgasm is explosive—mind-numbing—and everything goes black for a minute as I lose myself in the sensations.

"Fuck," I hear Oliver say from somewhere behind me. "As if I wasn't horny enough already."

"Good thing we have our own personal fuckdoll, isn't it?" Rhett says. Oliver chuckles.

"You want all three of us to fill you with our cum, Wren?"

"Yes," I moan.

Rhett rests his hands on my hips, guiding me as I start moving again. I ride him harder, bouncing up and down on his cock. He's watching me with a satisfied smirk, like he loves how desperate I am for the three of them.

"So needy." The words come from Elliot. His fingers brush across my upper back before he comes to stand in my line of sight. "You fuck him so well, love."

I stretch upward with a little whine, reaching out for him. Elliot leans down, running a hand over my hair before kissing me gently.

"I could watch you two like this all day," Oliver says. He kneels next to Rhett, kissing him before turning to watch me. "So goddamned hot."

"Shit," Rhett groans. "Don't stop, Wren."

My legs are getting tired, but the look on Rhett's face pushes me to keep going. The pride I feel knowing I'm the reason behind his groans is indescribable. And when Rhett comes, I smile to myself at the way he throws his head back with a grunt.

Over the past couple weeks, I've come to revel in the rare moments in which I see Rhett completely uninhibited. I don't catch it often. But those times—right after he's woken up, or when he thinks no one is watching him, or when he comes—are ones I'll always pay special attention to. Seeing Rhett let down his walls, even if it's only for a millisecond, is a beautiful thing.

There are a lot of things I have yet to learn about him—why he seems averse to vulnerability, the reasons behind his insomnia, what exactly happened with Sammy, et cetera. I have a feeling it's all connected and that it'll be a long and painful conversation for him. Maybe that's why I haven't asked yet. The look in his eyes whenever Sammy gets brought up is one of excruciating pain.

Once Rhett has come down from his high, Elliot loops his arms under mine and pulls me up. He turns me around and kisses me again, except this time his movements are hungrier.

When he releases me, he's smiling. "I'd say it looks like O and I got back just in time."

CHAPTER TWO

Oliver

I crawl on top of Rhett, straddling him and placing my hands on the floor on either side of his head. "I haven't seen you all day. Have a good nap?"

Rhett doesn't answer, yanking me down into a rough, hungry kiss. His hand wraps around my throat possessively, and goddamn, I've missed the feeling.

I slept late this morning, and by the time I got up, Rhett had just gone to bed. It's not the first time it's happened—and it won't be the last. Not only is our work schedule ever-changing, but when you throw in Rhett's insomnia, sometimes we go longer than we'd like without seeing each other.

Today, I'm just happy that Rhett actually got some sleep. It also meant that Elliot and I got to go to the movies with just the two of us and that Rhett and Wren got some one-on-one time. It was nice, but we were all disappointed we weren't together.

"I missed you," I say when Rhett breaks off our kiss, his hand still lingering on my throat.

"I'll make it up to you soon," he replies with a wink that absolutely melts my insides. "But first . . ." His gaze falls to Wren. "You'd better make good use of the time you have left with your princess before she goes back home."

Standing, I give Rhett a hand and pull him up. Then I turn to Wren, my eyes following the trail of cum leaking down her inner thigh.

"Ah ah, princess. That stays inside of you." Stepping up to her, I use two fingers to push Rhett's cum back inside of her. "We said we'd fill you up, didn't we?"

She arches a brow in a challenge. "I'm waiting."

Elliot chuckles. "As you wish, love."

Gently, he brings Wren to her hands and knees. We both strip, and he settles on his knees behind her, sliding into her with little resistance. The whimper Wren lets out is almost entirely drowned out by Elliot's groan.

As I watch him fuck her, I can't help but stroke myself. But it's not long before Rhett comes up behind me, slapping my hand away and grabbing my dick. His free hand wraps around my throat again, squeezing ever so slightly.

"Elliot," Wren cries when he rubs her clit. "Gentle, gentle."

Rhett snickers. "A little sore, sweetheart?"

She sobs in relief when Elliot pulls his hand away from her clit.

"Sore from what?" I ask.

"Let's just say she needed to be taught a lesson," Rhett murmurs darkly in my ear.

Elliot's eyes light up with amusement. Wren starts meeting his thrusts, pushing against him, and he smacks her ass.

"Oh, you want everything else rough, huh?"

Wren barely manages a nod.

Elliot obliges, thrusting into her hard. "Someday—someday *soon*—two of us are going to take you here at the same time." Slowly, he eases two fingers into her vagina along with his cock.

Wren falls to her elbows, screaming into the crook of her arm.

"What did I tell you about quieting your screams, love?" Elliot growls. Then he grabs the hair at the base of her neck and yanks her head up.

She places both her hands back on the mat, too breathless to reply, but she's smiling.

Rhett releases my dick and shoves me toward them. "The only thing that should muffle your cries is one of our dicks shoved down your throat, you understand?"

Her only response is a moan.

"Maybe you should show her what I mean, O." Rhett pushes me to my knees in front of her.

Wren's gaze turns greedy as she locks eyes with me. As soon as I'm within reach, she's sucking my dick with unrestrained enthusiasm.

"So eager for our cocks," I say, petting her hair. "Such a good whore."

I let her have control for a minute, my head falling back as she moves up and down on my dick. But then Elliot starts pounding into her even harder, forcing her forward enough that she chokes on my cock.

"You can take it," I say, grabbing onto her hair and thrusting forward in time with Elliot. "Goddamn, princess. You feel so good."

Wren hangs on for as long as she can before weakly slapping her hand against my thigh. I pull out, smiling down at her. She coughs, drool falling from her mouth before she takes a deep breath. Then she opens her mouth, sticking her tongue out for me.

"Ready and waiting," Rhett murmurs, his hand wrapping around my throat from behind. "Such a good girl."

I love that he can't stop touching me, I think as I slide back into Wren's mouth.

We aren't gentle with her. That's not what she wants. And Wren takes every thrust beautifully.

When she taps my thigh again, I pull out for longer and watch her. Her eyes are glazed over from the heady sensations, her muscles straining from the tension building in her body.

"Elliot," she moans.

"Come for us, love. Let yourself go."

I capture her chin in between my fingers. "Up here, princess. Look at me while you fall apart."

"Oli . . . Oliver—oh my *god*," she cries, her eyes closing as Elliot's ministrations pull her under.

"Look at me."

With a gasp, she returns my gaze. Her eyes are wild with pleasure, but she manages to keep them open per my command.

"Such a good girl." I smile down at her, stroking her face.

Elliot groans, grabbing onto Wren's hips. *"Fuck."* His grip on her tightens as he finishes.

I've always loved watching Elliot come. His entire body goes rigid, and he loses control of his calm, put-together facial expressions. And then he usually collapses, exhausted and sated.

As Elliot falls forward, he does his best not to crush Wren with his weight. He covers her shoulders and back in tiny, worshipful kisses while he recovers. "I swear, love, sometimes it feels like you were made just for the three of us."

Her response is a lazy smile directed toward me. When Elliot pulls out of her, she starts to move, but he holds her still.

"You're not going anywhere yet. That cum stays inside of you until we say so."

Wren settles back into position, leaning down so her ass is in the air and she's propped up on her elbows again. I kiss the top of her head before walking around her and settling in between her legs. Elliot and Rhett's cum is already leaking out of her, and I push it back in with my fingers.

"Give me more, Oliver," she pleads, and I can't help but laugh.

I line myself up with her entrance. Then, gently, I ease into her, my eyes closing at the feeling of her wrapped around my dick. "Fuck, princess. You feel like heaven."

What Elliot said is true. It feels like Wren was created to be the final person in our group. But it's more than that, really. All four of us fit together so eerily well despite all of our differences. So it's not just that Wren was made for us. It's that we were all made for each other.

I can't imagine wanting anyone other than them.

Rhett gets down to Wren's level, grabbing her face and fitting his mouth to hers in an all-consuming kiss. I move in and out of her slowly, letting myself enjoy the feeling.

Is there anything better than this?

Wren clenches around me with a groan.

Shit. Definitely not.

"Fuck yourself on my dick, princess. Give me all you've got."

She obeys without question, practically sobbing into Rhett's mouth. Her ass bounces against my hips repeatedly, and I have to say, the view is pretty damn good.

After a minute, I reach down and find her clit. It's a slightly awkward position, but I can make it work. As soon as I start stroking it gently, she begins to shake.

"You're so beautiful when you're like this," Rhett murmurs, his face mere inches from hers. "Fucked to complete oblivion."

She clamps down on me again, almost like she can't help herself. *Fuck.* If she keeps doing that, I'm a goner.

"I need you to come, Wren," I say tightly.

"You hear that, sweetheart? Better do as you're told if you don't want another punishment."

I rub her clit faster, doing my best to not apply too much pressure since she's sore. Apparently it's just what she needed. In under a minute, Wren cries out, her body convulsing as she comes. I let myself go, finishing inside her and filling her to the brim. When I pull out, she whimpers, and I spread her cheeks to get a better view of our cum dripping out of her.

"We should do this more often," I say, grinning at Elliot and Rhett.

Wren collapses onto the mat. She's a panting, sweaty mess, and she's never looked more like ours.

I get up, and the three of us stand over her like guardian angels. Actually, probably more like corruptive demons. *Protective* corruptive demons.

Crouching next to Wren, Elliot lifts her into his arms. "Let's get you cleaned up and soaking. We can't leave you feeling too sore."

. . .

While Elliot takes care of Wren, Rhett all but drags me into his room.

"You know," I say as he turns the shower on, "I would've come willingly."

"Don't pretend you don't like it when I manhandle you, O."

I can't help but smile. He's right.

Once the water is warm, Rhett pulls me into the shower and soaps me up. He does this whenever he can, and considering he can't keep his hands off me, I figured today wouldn't be the exception.

I relax as he scrubs me down with a washcloth. This is probably the only alone time I'll get with Rhett today, and I have no desire to do anything except bask in his attention.

"How was the movie?" he asks.

"All right. A lot of stupid stunt moves, but at least Ell and I laughed a lot. Wished you were there, though."

"I know." He pushes me under the spray of water. "But having Wren here when I woke up was probably for the best. Got in more training."

After she finished work this afternoon, Elliot picked her up and brought her here. She had the choice to either come to the movie with us or stay home and hang out with Rhett when he woke up. She chose the latter, saying she didn't want him to wake up alone, which I thought was really sweet.

Rhett finishes rinsing me off and then cleans himself. I'd offer to help, but I know he won't let me. So instead I take in the lines and curves of his body, watching the way his muscles flex as he runs his washcloth across his skin.

"Once we get back from this job, I want to do something nice for Wren," he says as he rinses off. "With all of us. Take her out on a date or something."

"Yeah?" I smile. Seeing Rhett care for her has hope blooming in my chest. Opening up to Wren has been hard for him, but he's doing the best he can, just like he does for me and Ell. It's been so long since he's let someone else in that I was beginning to think it'd never happen.

"I like it when she smiles."

This man is fucking adorable.

"And she's been stressed lately, I think," Rhett continues. "Makes sense considering everything we put her through last week. Plus the shit going down with her family. And Adam."

Rhett spits Adam's name out of his mouth with disgust. After last Tuesday when I found Wren unceremoniously beating her ex over the head with a book, Rhett has wanted to kill the guy. Almost did, actually, but Wren asked him not to. So Rhett let Adam move out of the city instead.

We're not exactly sure about the specifics surrounding Wren's family. She told us some stuff last week, but none of us want to push her into opening up before she's ready. Her family doesn't seem terribly supportive, though. More controlling than anything else.

"She seems a little lost," I say.

Rhett's gaze meets mine, and he nods. "The night at the cabin, after you were asleep, she said something to me. She's afraid of forgetting who she is again. I don't know what she meant—not sure *she* knows what she meant. She was freaking out and kind of rambling on. But I . . ." He works his jaw before sighing. "I don't know."

"What?"

"Remember what she told us about Adam? About how she made herself believe she wanted the future he wanted?"

"She's not doing that with us, Rhett. Don't even let your mind go there."

"What if she is? We jumped into this really fucking fast, O. How can she be okay with dating three paid killers without some serious thinking first? I get that she likes us. But when she agreed to this relationship, she didn't know what we are."

Despite the steam filling the shower, I suddenly feel cold. "What are you suggesting?"

"What if . . . I don't know, what if we're some type of rebound? If she's not sure what she wants from life, how the hell does she know she wants us? Are we just the first guys who gave her attention after Adam? Or maybe—"

"Rhett."

He pauses, looking at me expectantly.

I sigh. Honestly, I should've seen this coming. Out of all of us, Rhett has the most trust issues. With good reason, but I hate that he can't see what I'm seeing so clearly—Wren's feelings are completely genuine.

"First of all, we agreed to a *chance.* A chance that this could work."

Rhett looks away, his jaw tight. It's not what he wants to hear and I know it.

"But," I say slowly, reaching out and shutting off the water, "I'd say it's working pretty well. There have been a few hiccups, sure, but we've worked our way through them. And I know you may be worried that she stepped into this relationship for the wrong reasons, but I don't think so. Just watch her the next time she looks at one of us. That's not a rebound look."

"But why hasn't she freaked out yet? We kill people for a living, Oliver. *Murder* people."

I grin. "You're missing one key factor."

"What?"

"Wren is smart. Damn smart. I bet she'd already guessed what we were before we told her. And that probably eased her into it some."

"Maybe so," he mutters.

"Just trust this," I say, resting my hands on his shoulders. "And if you can't, then trust me."

He touches his forehead to mine, eyes closed, and breathes out a sigh. "Always, O. Always."

CHAPTER THREE

Elliot

Having Wren curled up in the tub with me is becoming one of my new favorite things. I prefer it when we exhaust her so thoroughly that she falls asleep and I get to bring her to bed with me, but I know that can't happen tonight. Wren opens at the shop tomorrow. It's a long drive from here to there, and she prefers not to have to make it in the morning.

We're also leaving late tomorrow morning for Middle-of-Nowhere, Wyoming, and we still need to finish packing. We didn't want to take the job, but the woman who hired us is powerful. The type of person you want as an ally. There's a saying among the people who know her—there are no secrets in Philadelphia. Because if you have one? Sparrow Belgrave knows it. She has eyes and ears fucking everywhere.

Taking this job puts us on her radar. And hopefully, when we succeed without a problem as we always do, it'll gain us a bit of her trust. Then when the time is right and we need to buy information, she'll happily sell.

Wren turns her head slightly, looking up at me. "I'm going to miss you."

"I know, love," I murmur, kissing the top of her head. "You're sure you want to stay home?"

She nods.

I bite back the ten replies that rush to the front of my mind, all of which are different ways to convince her to come with us. If she doesn't want to, that's up to her. And odds are, she'll be perfectly safe here. With Finn watching her back, no one will be able to get within ten feet of her.

"Can I ask you a question about Rhett?" she says quietly.

"Can't guarantee I'll answer, but go for it."

"Should I ask him about Sammy? And about why he's so . . ."

"Closed off?"

She nods. "I want to know. But I don't want to push him before he's ready to open up about it."

"I don't think he'll ever be ready, love."

She sags against me with a sigh. "I understand that."

I squeeze her lightly. Reliving his past is a nightmare for Rhett. His mom passed from cancer not long after Sammy was born. Rhett's dad put him through hell before her death, and it only got worse after. And then Sammy was killed, and Rhett was absolutely done with his father. He moved in with me and my parents for the remainder of our senior year.

To this day, Oliver and I don't even know the extent of abuse that Rhett went through. Just what he's decided to share.

There are things Wren needs to know. At some point, she should know everything that Oliver and I do. But it'll be slow going for Rhett. You can't force trust.

We stay in the bath for a few more minutes. After I help her out of the tub, she presses her body into mine. We're both dripping a ton of water onto the bath mat, but I don't care. Any shred of closeness I can get to her, I'll take.

"Thank you for taking care of me," she says.

I brush a hand down her back. "It's the bare minimum, love."

Wren places a tender kiss to my chest before we dry off and get dressed. As much as I want to keep her all to myself for as long as I can, it's not fair to the other guys. We only have tonight to be with her, and I love them too much to be selfish.

Downstairs, Rhett and Oliver are in the kitchen. Oliver hands Wren a bowl of chocolate chip cookie dough ice cream, planting a kiss on her lips as he does.

"What's this for?" she asks with a smile, popping a spoonful into her mouth.

"Tradition," Oliver says. "We always have ice cream the night before a job. Helps with the jitters."

Wren raises an eyebrow. "Ice cream before, sex after. Any others?"

"You'll have to wait and see," I say, taking my own bowl from Rhett. "For now, just enjoy."

We settle in the living room. I sink into one of the armchairs facing the couch, where Wren sits down with Rhett and Oliver on either side of her. Rhett hasn't said a word since we came down, and he seems more pensive than usual.

Maybe he's still tired.

Sneaking an arm around Wren, Oliver balances his ice cream bowl in his lap. "Five."

"Five?" she asks.

"Five orgasms a day."

A slow smile creeps onto Wren's face. "Can you come that much in a day?"

"Not for me, princess. For you. I promise I'll give you *at least* five orgasms a day on this trip if you come with us."

"Oliver," I scold. "She already said no."

Wren hides her giggles by taking another bite of her ice cream. "It's a little late for me to change my mind. You guys are leaving while I'll still be at work."

He pouts, but she kisses him, and when she pulls away he's grinning.

"You're still visiting me before you leave, right?" Wren asks, glancing at the three of us. Rhett watches her intently as she does so, which I think is a little odd, but whatever.

"Of course," I say. "What would Friday mornings be without coming to the coffee shop?"

"Miserable," Oliver says. "You're my favorite part of Fridays."

"Wow," Rhett says, cutting him a teasing look. "I'll make sure to tell your mom that the next time we see her."

Oliver's eyes widen. "Fuck."

Every Friday, we have lunch with Oliver's mom. Our cover is that we work in finance. So on Fridays, we "take a half day" to catch up with her. Sometimes Oliver's sister joins, too. Obviously we're skipping tomorrow, but we try to prioritize it when we can. Out of all our family, Oliver's mom and sister are the only ones we're consistently in contact with.

I explain that all to Wren, and she can't hold back a smile. "So that's why you guys are always in suits when you come in?"

Oliver nods. "Gotta act the part. What kind of financial advisers would we be if we weren't in suits?"

"Investment bankers," Rhett corrects.

Waving his hand dismissively, Oliver says, "Same thing."

I chuckle. "Definitely not."

"You know who doesn't know the difference?" Oliver says, winking at Wren. "My mom."

For the next hour or so, we hang out together, our conversation flowing with a relaxed ease that has me wishing tonight would never end. These are the kinds of moments I'll never get enough of. Getting to explore the thoughts of these three is one of my favorite pastimes.

But unfortunately, it's getting late. Wren is yawning every couple minutes. When she glances at the clock on the mantel, her expression saddens.

"It's time?" Rhett says.

She nods.

"I'll take you home," he mutters.

Wren turns to Oliver, leans over, and kisses him. When she pulls away, he grabs her and hauls her onto his lap. He kisses her again, holding onto her tightly, and she doesn't resist. Eventually, Wren breaks off the kiss with a reluctant sigh.

"Text me when you can?"

He nods. "We will. But we'll be without service for a couple of days. No internet either for the most part."

"I'm going to miss you." She turns in Oliver's lap, glancing to me and Rhett. "All of you."

I stand, opening up my arms, and she enters them after giving Oliver one last longing look. I bury my face in her hair, inhaling the sweet scent of her shampoo.

Everything in me wants to promise that we'll be back in a few days, but I can't get her hopes up. There's a chance this could take all week. So instead I kiss her temple and squeeze her shoulders.

"Remember that Finn will be walking you to and from work," I say. "And if you see anything even remotely suspicious, please—"

"I'll call him," she says. "I promise. But I'm sure I'll be fine."

"You will be," I say firmly, mostly to convince myself, but also because there's a hint of worry in her voice.

Goddammit. I wish she was coming with us. Finn is perfectly capable of keeping her safe, but I'd prefer to do it myself. Giving up control isn't my area of specialty.

When I finally let Wren go, it feels like I'm making a fatal mistake. But it's not like I can force her to come with us.

"Don't forget to grab your water bottle from the gym," Rhett tells Wren.

"Oooh! I almost forgot. I'll meet you in the garage."

After she leaves the room, Rhett turns to Oliver.

"The way she looks at us." It's an acknowledgment of something, but I'm not sure what. Doesn't matter—it sounds like it's between the two of them.

Oliver smiles up at him. "Yeah?"

Rhett stares at the floor. "You were right."

Gently, Oliver takes Rhett's hand in his. He brings it to his lips, kissing each knuckle reverently. "I know it's hard for you. I'd never pretend it's not. But you can trust this. I promise it's safe to."

The wave of emotions that crosses over Rhett's face takes me aback. He usually keeps his facial expressions under lock and key, but right now, I can see everything.

"Thank you," he mutters, pulling Oliver into a kiss. Then, "I'll be back soon. I love you both."

We both stand in stunned silence as Rhett disappears through the doorway. I can't remember the last time I heard those words from his mouth. Not that I'm complaining, and not that I don't know. I just wasn't expecting it.

"He's okay, right?" I ask.

"Yeah," Oliver replies. Then he smiles. "Maybe even a little better."

. . .

When Rhett gets back, it's been an hour and a half, but we haven't left the living room. I'm on the couch in front of the lit fireplace, and Oliver is sprawled out with his head in my lap, snoring softly.

Quietly, Rhett grabs the blanket from the back of the couch and places it over Oliver's body. Then he kisses me on the forehead, his lips lingering against my skin. When our gazes meet, it's only for a split second before he turns away, but it's still enough to catch the glimmer of guilt in his eyes.

Rhett hasn't always had insomnia. It started the year after Sammy was killed, and it's come and gone ever since. It's worrisome, and it's one of the many reasons I'm looking forward to putting Ludo behind us. I can't help but hope that once we've avenged Sammy's murder, it'll give Rhett some of the peace he needs. I also can't help but worry that it won't help, and Rhett will forever be stuck in the endless cycle of pain, grief, and anger that he's been in for the past decade.

"He understands," I remind him, stroking a hand down Oliver's arm. He's stopped snoring, but based on his breathing pattern, he's still out.

Rhett watches us both, the light from the fireplace casting half of him in warmth and the other half in shadow. Then he shakes his head. "He shouldn't have to miss a person he lives with. I should've waited until tonight to get some sleep."

"He'd rather you get the rest. God knows you need it."

"Well, *I* would rather have more time with the people who mean the most to me."

"If we're talking about what we want," Oliver mutters sleepily, "I'd love for you to fuck me."

I snort, and Rhett rolls his eyes.

"But," Oliver continues, "if we're talking about the grander scheme of things, I can start staying up later to see you more."

"No," Rhett says. "Sleep is important, O. You need it."

"Say that again."

"You need it."

Oliver groans. "The other part."

"Sleep is important."

"Exactly."

"Fuck you," Rhett grits out.

"You make it sound like it'd be a punishment."

With a dark smirk, Rhett says, "If that's how you want it."

I laugh, shaking my head. "Not now. You'll fall asleep before he even gets his dick half inside you."

Oliver groans in acknowledgment that I'm right. "Wren get home okay?"

Rhett exchanges an amused glance with me. "Obviously."

"Gotta keep her safe," Oliver mumbles.

The room falls quiet. None of us like that we're leaving her alone, even with Finn keeping an eye on her. Hell, I don't like her sleeping at her apartment alone, even though it's perfectly safe there. But it's not like we can ask her to move in with us. It hasn't even been two weeks since we added her to our relationship.

"Fuck." Oliver sits up, seemingly much more awake than he was seconds ago. "Ludo was watching her. At Evolve that night, when I left her alone for a minute. I didn't like the way he was looking at her."

Rhett goes stiff. "What do you mean, *he was watching her?* How? In what way? And why didn't you say something before now?"

"I forgot, honestly. He was looking at her like he was . . ." Oliver hesitates, probably worried about what Rhett's reaction will be. "He looked interested in her."

Rhett mutters a few choice words under his breath before he starts pacing. His body is riddled with tension. "I don't want her anywhere near him."

"None of us do," I say.

Shaking his head, Rhett turns to face us. "You know how Ludo can get. He's fucking sick. And if he has Wren in his sights—no. Just no. We have no idea what could be going through his head. What he wants."

The three of us lapse into silence. Ludo is known for many things, but some of the more prominent rumors are ones that delve into his darker side. He loves killing—capturing his victims, toying with them, and enjoying their long, slow, helpless deaths. It's also been said that he's killed multiple of his romantic partners. Whatever reasons he has for taking up interest in Wren, none of them are good.

"What are you suggesting?" Oliver asks.

"We need to wrap this up quicker than originally planned."

Another silence. Oliver and I watch Rhett carefully.

We were all heartbroken when Sammy was killed, but of course Rhett took it the hardest. He's the one who came up with the idea of revenge. Oliver and I are completely on board, but ultimately this is for Rhett. If he wants to change things up, then we'll follow. *As long as* he's thinking straight.

Oliver breaks the silence. "To keep Wren out of danger?"

Rhett nods. "I've said in the past that I want to make Ludo suffer. I still do, and I still will. But priorities change. If Ludo has any kind of interest in Wren, I want him to get what he deserves as soon as possible. Sammy will still get her justice. But Wren will be safe, too."

My mind instantly jumps into planning mode, going through all the possibilities of how we can switch up our current strategy. The idea is to tear down Ludo's empire, to make him feel as helpless as we felt all those years ago. And then, when he's at his lowest and he's suffered enough, we'll kill him.

"You're sure you won't regret it?" Oliver says.

Rhett works his jaw. "No. But I *do* know that I'll regret drawing this out if Wren ends up hurt in the process. If she was better trained and we knew she could protect herself, then it would be a different story. But that's not the case. And I don't trust Ludo to stay away from her even though he knows she's with us."

"Timeline?" I ask.

"Six months max."

"Fuck, Rhett."

Our current plan for Ludo's demise still has two years left. The idea was to draw his pain out for as long as possible. Some of it can be squeezed into a shorter time frame, but not all of it.

"I'm willing to sacrifice certain things," Rhett says. "Mostly I just want him to feel pain. And then I want him dead."

"Okay. I can start re-thinking things when we get back from this job. As long as—as long as you're *sure,* Rhett. You've been waiting a decade. We all have. And once he's gone, you can't take it back."

"I need to know Wren will be safe. And until Ludo is dead, I can't guarantee that. So yes—I'm fucking positive."

Oliver lets out a relieved breath. "I wouldn't mind being able to move on by the end of the year."

I nod in agreement. We all mourned Sammy's death when we were teens, but that's the thing about death. You never truly stop grieving. And while we're making sure Ludo pays for what he did all those years ago, drawing out the process has been its own special kind of pain.

"Six months," Oliver murmurs.

I nod, my thoughts racing.

"Six months," Rhett says, glancing between the two of us. "Six months, and then we're done."

Chapter Four

Rhett

Friday morning, the coffee shop isn't terribly busy. I find myself checking the exits repeatedly, like doing so now will somehow protect Wren while we're gone. Thankfully, Oliver and Ell are too busy watching Wren work to notice.

Jesus. We're all fucking wrecked for this woman.

I sip on my black coffee while looking around the shop again. Everything is exactly the way it always is. I know I'm just being paranoid. But ever since Oliver told us that Ludo was watching her the other night, I've been on edge.

Wren catches my eye and smiles. I freeze.

Just watch her the next time she looks at one of us. That's not a rebound look.

Oliver was right. Last night, I made sure to watch Wren more closely, and the way her eyes lit up or her gaze softened whenever she looked at one of us had my heart aching. I never should've doubted her. Trusting people just . . . doesn't come easily to me.

"We should get going soon," Elliot says reluctantly.

I tear my gaze away from Wren. Six months. Six months, and then all of this will be over, and we'll never have to leave her again.

None of us really knows what life will look like after Ludo is dead. Will we still take on jobs? I don't know. It's not like we need the money. We're taking them now because of reputation and connections reasons. But in the future, I'd like to know that Ell, Oliver, and Wren are safe. Our lifestyle doesn't lend itself to that kind of security easily.

Once we've finished our coffee, we stand. Wren comes around the counter, giving Elliot and Oliver lingering hugs and quick kisses. When she turns to me, I sweep her up into my arms and press my face into her hair.

"I'll see you soon," she says. "Stay safe."

"Always." I kiss her. And then I kiss her again, this time more deeply, a secret apology for my doubts last night.

She looks a little flustered as I pull away—maybe even a little embarrassed. When I look around, I see why. Multiple other customers are watching the four of us. Some curiously, some judgmentally. A single look from me, and they immediately go back to minding their own damn business.

As we leave the coffee shop, I look back. Wren is watching us from behind the counter. She waves, and I nod. And when the door shuts behind me, I can't help but shake the feeling that I'm leaving a very vital part of me behind.

. . .

One of the many benefits of having access to a private plane is not having to deal with nearly as many people. It makes the whole boarding process a lot easier, and I'm able to relax more on the flight.

Once we're in the air, Elliot pulls out his laptop. "I just have some things I want to go over."

"I should probably try to catch up on sleep," I say. I tried to rest last night, but I wasn't able to. Typical.

"I'll come too," Oliver chirps. "To help you relax."

Elliot rolls his eyes and laughs, not looking up from his laptop as we move into the bedroom.

I flop onto the bed stomach down, hiding my smile in the pillows when Oliver crawls on top of me and straddles my ass. His hands move to my shoulders, massaging, and I can't help but groan. He works me for a few minutes, focusing on the knots in my shoulders before moving down my arms.

"You know you're supposed to relax when someone's giving you a massage, right?"

"I am relaxed."

"Jesus Christ. Your muscles are literal rocks," Oliver says.

"They're not the only thing that's hard," I grumble.

With a deep chuckle, Oliver leans down until his lips are hovering right by my ear. "Good."

"I meant your ass. It's bony as hell."

With a disbelieving huff, Oliver crawls off and pushes me until I'm flipped over and lying on my back. He stares pointedly at my cock.

"Okay. Maybe that, too."

Before he can make a smartass remark, I grab him and pull him onto the mattress next to me. He grins, that familiar mischievous glimmer in his eyes. It's a playful look I've come to love over the years. But right now, being playful is the last thing on my mind.

Rolling on top of him, I pin Oliver to the bed. He groans when I fit my mouth to his, my hands keeping his wrists in place. Ell may love tying Oliver up, but I much prefer to hold him down myself.

"Fucking hell, Rhett," Oliver gasps when I move my lips to his neck, attacking the spot that always makes him go wild. He moves to touch me, but I keep his arms pinned down.

"You want me to fuck you?"

"Obviously," he grunts, craning his neck for another kiss.

"Then be a good boy and stop struggling."

That causes Oliver's face to light up with a grin. He relaxes, and I reward him with my lips moving against his. I let go of one of his wrists, grabbing onto his throat and squeezing. I add the amount of pressure he likes. It's a firm grip, but it's not so tight that he'll pass out.

With his free hand, Oliver fumbles with my pants, trying to undo them. "Fuck, why is this button being so goddamned—there! Finally." He yanks down my zipper before reaching into my boxers and grabbing my dick.

Groaning, I thrust into his palm. Having him on top of me had me so hard I was almost grinding into the mattress. But the feeling of his fingers wrapped around my cock makes it worth the wait. Still, it's not enough.

I lean down to kiss him again, and he meets my movements with unrestrained enthusiasm.

More. I need more.

With a grunt, I yank myself off of Oliver. He lets out a disappointed whine, but I'm already tearing his shirt over his head. Then I kiss him again, like I can't fucking stop myself. Because I *can't*.

He pulls away. "If you're not inside of me in the next five minutes, I'm going to get Ell to fuck me."

"Like hell you will," I growl.

"Watch me," Oliver says indignantly as he starts to move to the edge of the bed.

I let him go for a second because I know what he wants, and god-dammit, I want it too. But before he's even off the mattress, I grab the waistband of his pants and jerk him back.

"Who said I wouldn't?"

Oliver snickers.

"But I'm a selfish bastard, O, and I want you to myself first."

"Then fuck me already, you tease."

"With pleasure," I say, my tone conveying my unspoken words: *don't expect me to be gentle.*

I yank Oliver's pants and boxers off in one go. Then I haul him up so he's on his hands and knees. "One second."

I rifle through my bag, looking for some lube. Once I find it, I crawl onto the bed behind Oliver, spreading his cheeks and squirting some of the lube onto my fingers. When I brush one over his asshole, he jumps.

"Cold," he complains.

"You're fine," I chide.

I take my time prepping Oliver, making sure he's nice and ready. Besides, I like making him wait. He's fun to tease.

After lubing up my cock, I rub it against his hole. He groans in frus-tration, trying to push back against me, but I smack his ass.

"Now, Rhett," he grits out.

"Didn't you ever learn that patience is a virtue?"

"Please."

With a smirk, I slide into him. It's just an inch or two, but the moan that leaves his mouth has me giving him more. Every whimper and gasp that I pull from Oliver is like a small victory. I devour them, driving into him harder, the sounds only making me want more.

"Fuck," Oliver shouts.

I slap his ass, not slowing my pace. "Keep it down, the fucking pilot probably heard that."

Oliver lets out another loud moan, and then I hear movement outside the bedroom.

"That doesn't sound like sleeping to me," Elliot says from the doorway.

"Get in here and shut him up."

With an amused huff, Elliot closes the door and sheds his clothes. He climbs onto the bed in front of Oliver, bending down to kiss him before straightening.

"Suck," Elliot says, shoving his dick in Oliver's face.

Oliver wastes no time wrapping his lips around Elliot's cock. He's still moaning, but not nearly as much, which makes me think he was only being that loud to get Ell's attention.

Can't say I'm disappointed, though.

"Christ," Elliot groans. His eyes lock with mine as Oliver does all the work, and then he's leaning forward and grabbing my face. When his mouth meets mine, it's more of a battle for dominance than a kiss.

Elliot pulls away first, his mouth still open, so I spit into it. He swallows with a smile. Then he grunts when Oliver sucks one of his balls into his mouth.

"Flip him over," I say, pulling out. We both grab Oliver and turn him so he's on his back.

"Shit," Oliver pants when I slide back into him. He's holding onto his legs and spreading them apart for me. "Don't stop."

Elliot slaps his dick across Oliver's face. "You like being fucked like this, huh? Bet you wish Wren was here so she could suck your dick, too."

"Jesus. Yes."

"Well she's not here," Ell says, "and you're supposed to be sucking *my* dick."

Oliver jumps back to work with a grin. I can feel myself getting close, so I slow down, not wanting to finish yet. Then I take Oliver's dick in my hand, moving up and down.

It's been a while since the three of us have fucked together without Wren. We've been busy, and adding her into our dynamic has been a hell of a lot of fun. I wish she was with us—I always do. But it's nice to connect with Elliot and Oliver, too.

Oliver lets out a telltale groan that I've heard a thousand times. Elliot pulls out of his mouth and strokes his own dick as he smirks down at Oliver.

"That didn't take very long, did it?" Elliot says in a mocking tone.

I move my hand faster, causing Oliver's eyes to roll into the back of his head. And then he finishes all over himself with a breathless moan.

It's rare that the sound of Oliver coming doesn't send me hurtling toward my own orgasm. "Oh, shit."

"Give it to me," Oliver pants. "Come on me. Please."

I pull out, and he wraps his hand around my cock. I'm not normally one to do as I'm told, but it only takes a few strokes before I'm doing exactly what Oliver requested and covering his stomach in my cum. It takes everything in me not to collapse on top of him once I'm done.

Oliver shimmies up the bed until his head is in between Elliot's legs. His tongue laves across Elliot's balls before he sucks on one. And it has Elliot swearing under his breath and moving his hand faster.

I chuckle. "Looks like you're not going to last long either, pretty boy."

"Shit," Elliot groans. "You're too fucking good at this, Ol."

It only makes Oliver work more enthusiastically. Within a minute, Elliot's eyes are squeezing shut as the tension in his body builds.

"Fuck," I whisper. Then louder, "Cover him in your cum, Ell. Don't make him wait."

Oliver moans in anticipation, and Elliot can't hold out any longer. He comes, letting out a loud groan as he does. Once he's finished, he falls on his side, panting.

"Jesus," Oliver says, staring down at himself. "That's a lot."

We all take a couple minutes to catch our breath. Then I head into the bathroom to wash my hands and grab a washcloth—maybe two or three washcloths. After cleaning up Oliver, I move to clean my dick, but he stops me.

"I've got it," he says. "You look like you're ready to fall over."

I am.

I collapse onto the bed, my eyelids too heavy to keep open. Oliver takes the washcloth and presses a kiss to my forehead. It's the last thing I remember before drifting off to sleep.

CHAPTER FIVE

Wren

When I get off my shift, Finn is waiting for me. This is my first time meeting him, but the guys showed me a picture of him so I know what he looks like.

I come around the counter with my bag, and he stands. The man towers over me even with his shoulders slightly hunched. Tattoos expand over almost every inch of his light skin. His dark hair falls into his face, which is the only un-tattooed part of him I can see. That paired with the fact that he's wearing all black makes him look intimidating as hell.

No wonder the guys wanted him looking after me.

"So *you're* Wren. Heard a lot about you."

I nod. "Nice to meet you."

He looks me up and down before shaking his head. "We'll see if you feel that way by the end of the week."

I'm about to ask what he means, but he's already halfway out the door. I scramble to keep up with him. He's silent the entire walk home, keeping a brisk pace that has me panting by the time we're walking into my apartment building.

In the elevator, he presses the button to my floor. Once the doors are closed, he turns to me, narrowing his eyes and tilting his head like he's deep in thought. "Shoulders back."

"What?"

"Keep your shoulders back," Finn says. "And don't stand with your feet so close together."

What the fuck?

I adjust my posture, straightening my spine and spreading my feet so they're shoulder-width apart. "Like this?"

"Get that questioning look off your face. Ruins the whole thing."

Seriously?

Crossing my arms over my chest, I say, "Listen, I appreciate you keeping me safe. But don't—"

"Oh, that's a much better expression. Crossing your arms helps too."

"What the hell are you talking about?"

"If I attacked you right now, would you be able to defend yourself?"

"N-no."

"Exactly. You don't know how to protect yourself. So until you do, your best defense is *appearing* like you could beat the shit out of anyone who even looks at you the wrong way. Act confident. Be intimidating. People will be more likely to leave you alone."

"Got it."

The elevator comes to a stop, and the doors slide open. We walk to my front door in silence, and I make sure to stand straight.

Finn does a quick sweep of my apartment while I take off my boots and coat. It's not until he's back in the main living area that I notice the present sitting on the counter.

"Did you put that there?" I ask, nodding to it.

Finn frowns. "Why the fuck would I get you a present?" Then he takes the box and shakes it. "This wasn't here when you left this morning?"

"No, I—"

"Oh! Oh, I know what this is. Elliot texted me about it. For you." Finn shoves the box into my hands.

I stare at the present, admiring the pretty dark red wrapping paper. "They got me a gift?"

"I think you know the answer to that. Now, I'm gonna get out of here. If that's a sex toy or something, I have no desire to be around when you pull it out of that box."

My body floods with heat. "Thanks for walking me home."

He nods. "You're not planning on going anywhere tonight? And I mean anywhere. Even if it's just a walk to get some fresh air."

"No, I'm staying in."

"Good. You should be perfectly safe in here." He points to my front door. "But if you step into that hallway, it should be with me by your side. Even if you're getting something from a fucking vending machine or going to the laundry room or whatnot. Your boys aren't paying me to watch over you in this tiny matchbox of an apartment, but if you leave, you're my responsibility. Got it?"

I nod, mind whirring. For some reason, I didn't realize they'd *hired* Finn to keep me safe. They made it sound like it was a favor or something.

"I'm staying close by," he says. "If you notice anything even remotely suspicious, call me. You won't be bugging me. Again, I'm getting paid very well for this."

"Got it. Call you if there's anything suspicious."

"Anything *remotely* suspicious."

"Or if I leave the apartment."

"Good to know you pay attention. See you in the morning." Finn makes sure the doorknob is locked before leaving.

Once I'm alone, I set the present on the kitchen counter and carefully unwrap it. Once I see what's inside, my heart skips a beat.

Where's my phone? Oh my god, where's my phone?

I run to my coat, searching the pockets until I find it. Then I scroll through my notifications, hoping I'm not too late.

Oliver: Just landed. Miss you already.

He sent it twenty minutes ago. They should still have service, right?

I hit the call button, praying that he'll pick up.

"Hey, princess. Everything okay?"

"Oliver!"

There must be something in my voice that clues him in to what I'm feeling, because he chuckles. The sound is warm and comforting, almost like he's here next to me. "I take it you got your gift."

"I don't even know what to say," I whisper, moving back to the counter.

"Ell made sure it's the same edition as your old copy. We know it can't really replace the one you had from high school, but—"

"Oliver. It's perfect."

Gently, I take the book out of its box. When Adam destroyed my copy of *A Tale of Two Cities,* I was heartbroken. This . . . this was so thoughtful of them.

"I'm glad you like it," Oliver says.

"I wish I could kiss you," I say, hugging the book to my chest. My heart feels so incredibly full.

Is this what it's like when people love you the way you need to be?

"Soon, princess. When we're back, you can kiss me as much as you want." There's a pause, and I hear one of the other guys say something I can't make out. Then, "Rhett says we have to share."

I giggle. "I think we can manage that."

Oliver can't stay on the phone, so we reluctantly hang up. I flip through the pages of my book, laughing when I see a note on the front page.

So you don't forget us.

"As if I ever could," I murmur.

After setting the book on the counter, I take a shower and then flop onto my bed. The past two weeks have taken their toll on me, and I'm exhausted. I need to eat, but my bed is so damn *comfy*. So I scroll through all the notifications on my phone, clearing most of them. There are only a couple that catch my eye—a missed call from my mom and two text messages.

Mom: We need to talk.

Mom: I wish you'd stop ignoring me.

I roll my eyes, swiping the notifications away. She still hasn't apologized for last Tuesday. Not only did she lie and say we'd be meeting for dinner alone, but she brought *Thomas*. A man she knows I have no desire to ever see again in my life. And it's not just that he was there, either. It was the whole damn intervention. I just want to live my own life the way I want to—whatever that ends up looking like.

After a couple more minutes in bed, my stomach growls ferociously, so I get up and toss a tank top and shorts on. Then, in the kitchen, I throw my phone onto the counter and start rummaging around for food. My gaze snags on the dishes Oliver took me shopping to get, and I can't help but smile. It was a sweet gesture.

I wish they were here with me right now.

With a sigh, I open up the fridge. The thought of cooking an entire meal sounds like way too much effort right now, but I really need to. It'll give me leftovers for the weekend.

Just as I start prepping some food, there's a knock on my front door. I freeze, a bag of baby carrots dangling from my hand. It's extremely rare that one of my neighbors needs something.

There's another knock. "Maintenance," a male voice calls out.

That's odd. I always get at least a twenty-four-hour notice if maintenance needs to get into the apartment.

Setting the carrots on the counter, I tiptoe to my door and peer through the peephole. The man is wearing a uniform, and he has one of the carts our maintenance guys use to lug stuff around, but that doesn't mean shit to me. I've read enough action novels to know how easy it is to get your hands on stuff like that.

I grab my phone to text Finn, but before I even have anything typed out, the man says, "It's an emergency, ma'am. I have a key from the building manager, and he said I have permission to come in if you're not home."

My heart skips a beat. The building manager is a *woman.*

This isn't good.

The doorknob jiggles, and I hear a key being inserted into the lock.

This is, in fact, very bad.

I give up on texting Finn and hit the call button.

He answers on the first ring. "Wren? Everything okay?"

"No, there's—" My chest squeezes as the man steps through the door.

"Put the phone down," he snaps. There's a gun in his hand now.

"Who is that?" Finn demands. "You're still at home?"

"Now," the man barks, pulling his shoulders back and standing at his full height—which is very, very tall.

I drop it just as he slams the door shut.

Finn's shouting voice sounds from my phone, but I can't make out what he's saying.

"What do you want?" Carefully, I back into the kitchen and move around the island so there's a barrier in between us.

"You'll do what I say, and you'll do it without questioning me."

Like hell I will.

There's no way he'll use that gun in here. There's no silencer attached, and it would be loud enough that half of the people in the building would probably hear and call the authorities. He'd never get away clean.

It's just an intimidation tactic—much like the ones Thomas uses. Maybe that line of thinking is stupid. But maybe it's what's going to get me out of this situation alive.

"You sound a lot like my stepdad," I say.

The man frowns.

"He thinks he's a lot scarier than he is, too."

Enraging my potential kidnapper-slash-murder is probably a bad idea. I think back to last Tuesday, to when Oliver told me I needed to work on my self-preservation instincts.

Fuck, maybe he's right.

"I don't have time for this shit," the man spits out. "You're coming with me."

He raises his gun, pointing it directly at my head. I don't move, instead crossing my arms and leaning against the counter behind me.

Finally—*finally*—I start to freak out. If he wants me to come with him, then at least he wants me alive. Whoever *he* is. But what happens after that?

Does he want revenge on the guys? Or is he going to use me as leverage for something? Or is it possibly not connected at all? And how the hell am I going to fight him off?

Rhett has only had the chance to go over basic self-defense moves with me. Going up against a man who looks like he's an enforcer of some type doesn't sound smart to me.

Before I can fully figure out what to do, he's moving toward me, shoving his gun into the waistband of his jeans. Panic floods my system when he pulls a syringe from his coat pocket.

"What is that?"

As he rounds the counter, I back away, grabbing the knife I was planning on using to cut up some vegetables. It goes against the advice Rhett gave me, but I'm counting on this guy wanting to keep me alive.

"Don't make this harder than it has to be."

"What, you think I'm just going to come willingly?" I make a slash at his arm when he reaches toward me, but I miss.

He grabs his gun again. "Put it down."

I freeze. *Shit. Is he actually going to shoot?*

He steps closer, and I realize that I've subconsciously lowered the knife a few inches.

Fuck. I have no idea what to do. Maybe I can—

He takes another step closer, and before I really think it through, I lunge forward. The knife cuts into his arm, but it barely phases him. Before I can pull back, I feel a sharp prick in my neck. He grabs my wrist and slams it against the counter.

The knife clatters to the floor as the first wave of drowsiness crashes over me. I stumble backward, but the man grabs me. My struggles are weak as the drug takes over. When my knees give out, he drags me toward the door.

The last thing I remember thinking is that I should've gone with the guys.

. . .

Harsh light filters through my eyelids, and I bring my hands over my eyes. I'm on a hard surface, and it feels like someone's been hitting my head with a hammer.

Where am I?

When I finally open my eyes, panic sets in.

I'm in an empty room, lying on the wood floor in a corner. The overhead light is on, which is killing my eyes, but I'm glad for it. Otherwise, I would've woken up in the dark.

Slowly, I climb to my feet, leaning against the wall for support. There are two windows on the one wall, but it's pitch-black outside, so I can't see where I am.

I move to the first of three doors in here. It leads to an empty closet, and the second to a small bathroom. I catch my reflection in the mirror, and I wince. I look like I've been through hell. And on top of that, there's blood on my tank top.

How the hell did that get there?

Back in what seems to be a bedroom, I try to open the third door. It doesn't budge, like it's locked from the outside.

Fuck. *Fuck.* What's going on?

"Let me out," I yell, wincing at the way it makes my head pound.

I try the door again, pulling harder, but it still doesn't move. With a groan, I sink to the floor and rest my head in my hands.

Think. Think! I was about to make myself dinner, and then . . . Nothing.

I hear movement below me. Voices—gruff, deep, and angry. Then the pounding of footsteps, coming higher, closer.

Shit.

As there's movement on the other side of the door, I scramble to my feet. When it opens, an angry man steps through, followed by two burly men dressed in all black. Something about the first guy is vaguely familiar, but I can't place how or why exactly.

"You're awake."

The world is spinning—I must've gotten up too fast. Carefully, I back up until I'm leaning against the far wall.

"Do you know who I am?" the man asks.

I shake my head.

He smiles, but there's nothing welcoming about it. "I know who you are. Wren Taylor, the unfortunate soul who happened to catch the attention of three men who, apparently, don't care enough to keep you safe."

I clench my fists behind my back. "Who're you?"

"Jordan Williams."

Williams. Edgar Williams' son?

No, Oliver said he didn't have any children.

Maybe another nephew?

"And what do you want, Jordan Williams?" Somehow I manage to keep the shaking in my voice to an imperceptible minimum. I'm honestly not sure how, because there's only one thing Jordan could want, and it has me feeling sick to my stomach.

"Your three boyfriends killed my brother. *And* my uncle, although I never cared much for the bastard."

I bite my lip, staying silent. Did the guys slip up somehow? Edgar and Tyler's deaths made the news, but the authorities said they were still trying to figure out who was behind it.

"Ask me how I know, Wren. Ask me how I know it was them."

"How?"

Jordan smiles at my obedience. "There are many people who wanted my uncle dead. His empire spans nations, and everyone wanted a piece of his power. But there's one man who would've benefited the most from my uncle's fall. His top competitor, especially in Philadelphia. Ludo Holloway."

"Sounds like a bit of a stretch." I shrug, hoping the bored expression I've crafted is working. Jordan's assumptions may be correct, but it doesn't sound like he *actually* knows—just that he's made some educated guesses. If I can convince him he's wrong . . .

"Ludo loves killing for sport. Everyone's heard the rumors by now. But when it comes to business, he doesn't mess around. You know who his go-to hitmen are?"

I shake my head, gulping when Jordan steps closer. His hot, stale breath hits my face as he laughs.

"I think you do, Wren."

"No."

"Your three boyfriends. They never fail, you know. And with a job like this, Ludo would've wanted a guaranteed kill. To be honest, if I was in Holloway's shoes, I would've hired them, too."

Dread weighs heavy on my chest, and it feels like I can barely breathe. "You want revenge."

"I don't just want it, Wren. I'll fucking get it."

"But if you know who ordered the kill on your brother," I say slowly, "why not get revenge on him?"

Jordan laughs. "You think I'm stupid? You think Ludo doesn't have three or more bodyguards with him at all times? That he's one of the smartest people on this goddamned planet? There's no way I can get to him.

"But you? Well, your boyfriends decided to publicly declare to the people in our world that you're theirs. And then they left you alone, completely defenseless. What was their logic? That no one would come after you this quickly?"

I almost laugh at my own stupidity. *No, that was* my *logic.*

Jordan continues, "Tyler stood to inherit everything that belonged to our uncle. But now that they're both dead, everything falls to me. Ludo thinks I'm an easy target. He's wrong. Any day now, he'll try to make a deal with me. He'll frame it as a *business arrangement.* Probably call it a *mutually beneficial agreement.* Do you think that's the truth, Wren?"

"No," I whisper.

"Good answer. He thinks I'm naïve. Gullible. He'll offer me a partnership, maybe even a mentorship. And then he'll try to pull the rug from underneath my feet. Do you think I'll let him?"

I know very little about Ludo Holloway, other than what the guys have told me. He seems ruthless, which has led me to believe that Elliot, Rhett, and Oliver are as well. I've seen them work, even if it was only a glimpse. And if they're going up against Ludo, they have to match—no, outmatch—who he is to defeat him.

As for Jordan, all I see is anger and insecurity. So yeah, I could easily imagine Ludo pulling one over on him. But I'm not stupid enough to say that out loud.

"Of course you won't."

Jordan grins. "Another good answer. Ludo thinks nothing of me now, but just you wait. He'll watch me take my place at the head of the

Williams empire. He'll watch me make it the greatest it's ever been. He'll regret ever killing my family. And more importantly, he'll regret ever underestimating me."

I shift from one foot to the other. I'd be lying if I said I cared about Jordan's plans to prove himself and to become more powerful. No, what I want to know is what he's going to do with *me*.

"You can't get revenge on Ludo, so you're going to . . . what, exactly? Kill me to get revenge on the guys?"

"Eventually. But they won't be walking away from this alive, either. I'll get them one by one and bring them here. How do you think they'll react when I drive a knife through your heart while I make them watch? Or when I hold your head under water until you pass out? I'll make them watch you die slowly from a lack of oxygen while they're helpless to stop me."

The weight on my chest is crushing me now—enough that I can't even respond. *They'll find me, right? Rhett said they would.*

"Now. Tell me why I texted Elliot an hour ago that I have his precious woman, and he hasn't even bothered to respond."

I hesitate. Should I tell him the truth? That Elliot isn't able to receive text messages? Maybe it'd buy me more time.

"They don't have service."

"What?" Jordan snaps.

"They're not in Philly."

"Fuck," he shouts. "That's not how this was supposed to work. Tell me where they went."

I shake my head.

"You really want me to start your torture early?" Jordan steps up to me, his arms crossed over his chest. "Because I will."

"I don't know where they are," I manage. "They didn't tell me."

Jordan's eyes narrow. "I don't believe you."

"It's the truth," I whisper.

"We'll see if you're still singing that same tune when I'm finished with you." Before I can reply, Jordan turns to face his men, pointing at me. "Grab her."

"No." I back into the far corner, but there's nowhere for me to run.

They each take hold of one of my arms, dragging me toward the bathroom. Jordan is already in there, plugging the bathtub and turning on the water.

"No," I screech, kicking at his men. Rhett hasn't taught me how to fight against two assailants yet, but I'm not above trying to figure it out on my own. I can't let them get me any closer to that tub.

"Calm her down," Jordan shouts over the running water, tapping his foot impatiently. "She's going to give me a headache."

One of them claps a hand over my mouth. His fingers cover my nostrils too, cutting off my air supply. It causes me to thrash around even more, trying to get free.

"Stay still," he growls in my ear, "and I'll let you breathe."

I bite his hand.

"Shit," he yells, yanking it away.

I spit his blood out of my mouth, jutting my elbow backward until it sinks into his stomach. But the other guy shoves me forward, and then I'm tripping and falling to my knees in front of Jordan.

He grabs my hair, yanking me to the tub's edge. There's already at least half a foot of water in it, and it's rising quickly. I try to scramble away, but he blocks me in.

"Record this," he says to his men. "I'll send it to Elliot. Fucker deserves it."

My next attempt to get away from the tub is met with Jordan grabbing me and shoving me down.

"No," I shout, holding onto the edge of the tub to steady myself.

Jordan knocks my hands away easily. I barely have time to get in air before my face is submerged in the water. Everything I do to try to get my head above the surface is met with Jordan holding me down more.

When he finally lets me up, I gasp for air.

"Where are they?"

"I don't know," I insist.

I'm only able to get in one breath before he shoves me down again.

The water is freezing, and Jordan is pushing my body into the edge of the tub in a painful way. I try to brace my hands on the opposite side and push myself back, but someone grabs my arms and wrenches them behind me.

No, no, no. I need air. I need—

Jordan yanks me up. I gulp in air as water streams from my hair down my body, soaking my clothes. Standing, Jordan knocks me to the ground.

"Maybe once they get these videos," Jordan grumbles, "your men will think twice before crossing a Williams."

"Fuck you," I manage in between coughs.

Jordan doesn't acknowledge me. "Keep her locked in here. And get me a different tub. It's too fucking crowded in here."

CHAPTER SIX

Oliver

I stare at my phone, willing one of the little bars in the top corner to light up. Talking to Wren over the phone after we landed this afternoon was nice, but it just made me miss her more.

This is going to suck.

We lost service minutes after my conversation with Wren ended, and we probably won't get it back until we're headed to the airport after the job is done. With a sigh, I shut my phone off. No sense wasting the battery.

Currently, we're in our cabin studying up on the ski resort our mark is staying at. It's fancy as hell, like the places Elliot's parents used to take us to during winter break. It reminds me of how easily the three of us could've never crossed paths—and makes me all the more grateful that we did.

Elliot went to prestigious private schools his entire life. Rhett and I, on the other hand, were in the public school system for most of our childhood. We both ended up at Elliot's academy freshman year on scholarships. We've always joked that it was a mistake that I got one since I wasn't the best at academics, but I like to think it was fate making sure we were together.

The three of us became fast friends, and since Elliot's family was loaded, they always brought us on their winter vacations. Mr. and Mrs. Hayes would let us do whatever the hell we wanted, and it was a blast. I never thought I'd get to learn how to ski or snowmobile or any of that shit. To this day, we always make a point to ski a couple times every winter. We're not pros by any means, but we don't suck, either.

I glance at Rhett from where I'm sitting at the kitchen table. After we had sex, he passed out immediately and stayed asleep for the entire flight. He volunteered to drive after we landed, which honestly was a relief. Elliot looked exhausted, and the last thing I wanted to do was drive in an unfamiliar place. With or without my anxiety meds—which I'm back on after a conversation with Rhett, Elliot, and Wren—driving has always made me nervous.

When I move my gaze to Elliot, I find him frowning over a map on the table. He looks up when he feels his eyes on me.

"You good?" I ask.

He nods. "Just trying to figure out a way to get home sooner."

That'd be nice.

Elliot points to a map of the resort's cross-country ski trails. "I scoured his social media and found what looks like a pattern. Every day he's out here, he posts a similar set of photos—his skis, the sunrise from the trails, and his breakfast at the resort. Must use the resort's Wi-Fi, because there's no damn way he has service out here."

I sigh, looking around. *I wish our cabin had Wi-Fi. Then we could talk to Wren.*

"How much people post publicly on the internet will never cease to amaze me," Rhett grumbles. He's been grouchy ever since he woke up.

"To be fair," I say, "the average person doesn't have to worry about someone following them across the country to kill them."

Absentmindedly, Elliot runs his thumb across his bottom lip. My guess is he didn't even hear what Rhett and I said. "He likes to get out in the early mornings. Probably has a light snack, hits the trails during sunrise, and then has a big breakfast at the resort's restaurant."

I lean forward. "So he'll be alone."

"And completely vulnerable," Rhett adds.

"Exactly," Elliot says. Then he points to a spot on the map. "All the trails start here. There are eight of them—three for beginners, three for intermediate skiers, and two for advanced skiers."

I groan. "How are we supposed to watch over eight trails?"

"Captions," Elliot mutters, tracing his finger along one of the black lines on the map.

"What?"

He stays silent for another moment.

I can't help but smile as I watch him. The way Elliot's brain works is fascinating to me. He's almost always calculating something, even if it's in the back of his mind. It's like life is a chess game to him, and he's always got five different strategies going while determining what moves will put him at the best advantage. Or however it works. I suck at chess.

"His captions. He usually says which trail he takes in his posts. There's no pattern—looks like he decides on a whim. But he never takes the easy trails, and he always avoids one of the advanced ones."

"That's still four trails," Rhett says. "And there are only three of us."

"Yes. But some of the trails join at certain parts. Like here." Elliot points to a spot on the map. "If we place ourselves strategically, then one of us should be able to get to him. And we have the radios to communicate."

I perk up. "We could do this tomorrow morning."

That gets Rhett's attention, too. He glances between me and Elliot. "Seriously?"

Slowly, Elliot nods. "No guarantees. Odds are, this guy will be out on the trails early tomorrow. But his routine could change. We may have to wait."

"So if this goes the way we want it to, we'll kill him tomorrow," I say. "And then what? Be on a flight out of here ASAP?"

"Depends on what the airport can manage," Elliot says. "We'll probably have to wait a while."

"I don't care. It's still way better than how long we thought we'd be out here originally."

"Agreed," Rhett murmurs.

We wanted to give ourselves time—thought this job could take up to a week. But since Elliot was able to find so much information on this guy's schedule online, things are looking up.

We could be home to Wren in a day.

For a couple more minutes, we talk through some details. But then we end our planning session early. We're going to need to get up before the sun in the morning, especially since we're going to have to scout out good hiding spots.

"If we can get home by tomorrow night, I'm not passing up that chance," Elliot says, standing from the table. He kisses me and then Rhett. "C'mon. Let's get some sleep."

CHAPTER SEVEN

Wren

I stay inside the empty room all night. At some point while it's still dark outside, I wake up crying from a nightmare. The light is still on, but it barely helps with the fear.

Saturday morning, I stare out the windows, trying to figure out where I am. I can't see much except a small front yard, a gravel driveway, and loads and loads of snow-covered trees. So probably the middle of nowhere.

Fuck.

I didn't get much rest last night. Not only is this floor really damn uncomfortable, but it's freezing in here. If I was in more than shorts and a flimsy tank top maybe I'd be fine, but they didn't even give me a blanket.

Sometime in what I think is mid-morning, the door to the bedroom opens and two men step in. Well, one man and one kid who looks like he's barely a legal adult. Panic fills my chest as they back me into a corner before grabbing my arms.

"Leave me alone," I shout, trying to yank myself from their grasp.

It's no use. This time, they drag me down two flights of stairs and into a dark, damp, unfinished basement. They take me into what looks like a cellar. There's a single light bulb hanging from the ceiling, illuminating a stainless steel trough of some sort. It's filled with water.

They dump me in front of it, and my knees hit the concrete floor. Pain shoots through my legs, but I try to get to my feet anyway. It's no good—they shove me back down in a split second.

"The more you struggle," Jordan says as he steps into the light, "the harder you'll make it on yourself." He taps the screen of his phone, which is on a stand with the back camera pointed this way. "How many videos do you think we'll be able to make before I get to them? How do you think they'll feel while they watch you almost drowning over and over again? I think they'll feel pretty helpless."

"Don't," I plead.

"Don't almost drown you? What, you'd prefer I kill you now? No, no. They'll be here in person for that."

One of the men grabs my arms and yanks them behind my back. The other secures my wrists together with a zip tie, tightening it so much that it digs into my skin.

"So you don't try to push yourself up the way you did last night," Jordan says. Then he kneels behind me, pressing his body into mine until I'm right up against the trough.

"How could you be so cruel?" I whisper.

It's the last thought I have before Jordan shoves my head into the freezing water. I try to twist out from underneath him, but he pushes me into the trough harder. The edge is much thinner than the tub upstairs, and the added pressure makes it dig into my body painfully.

Not struggling feels like giving up, but I didn't miss what Jordan said. Making this harder on myself is a stupid move. So I stay still, focusing on holding my breath.

Jordan pulls me up. "You're learning. Now look at the camera."

I do as he says, coughing and gasping.

"Look at her," Jordan shouts. "Soaked to the bone, freezing, and half-drowned. This is what happens when you fuck with the wrong people. I hope you learn your lesson."

Say something. Anything to give them a clue.

I take a deep breath, already anticipating that Jordan's going to put me back under for this. Then I say, "I'm in a house sur-"

I don't get to finish the sentence before my head is submerged in the cold water. Jordan keeps a tight grip on my hair, holding me underwater for longer than before. My lungs start to burn as my body is overcome with the desperate need to breathe anything in.

Just as I'm beginning to wonder if Jordan changed his mind and he's going to kill me now, he pulls me up. Relief floods me as I take in as much air as I can.

Three more times he shoves my head under water, keeping me there until my body is so deprived of oxygen, I feel dizzy.

"Put her back in her room," Jordan says, standing and letting me go.

I sway, but before I fall, his men are dragging me to my feet. They take me upstairs and lock me away, leaving me shivering and dripping onto the floor. At least they cut the zip tie off my wrists before they go.

So cold.

In the bathroom, I do my best to squeeze as much water out of my hair as possible. Then I wring out my clothes before putting them back on. I'd take them off to let them air dry, but I don't want Jordan or his men walking in on me naked.

I curse myself for putting on such little clothing yesterday. And then I rack my brain, trying to find any memory of last night. Did I leave the apartment without Finn? Or did someone break in? I have no idea.

My body aches, and I feel a little lightheaded. Plus I'm fucking starving. I didn't eat after work, so all I've had in the past day was the granola bar I scarfed down on my way to work yesterday morning.

Water. I should drink water.

My only option is from the bathroom sink. It tastes different from what I'm used to, like it's well water, not city water.

How far from home am I?

I glance out the windows. It's snowing.

I bury my face in my hands. Even if I managed to get away, it's freezing out there. I don't even have shoes, let alone a coat. I'd probably die from exposure in a matter of hours, especially considering I'm soaked. Hell, it probably wouldn't even take that long.

Pushing the thought away, I focus on getting warm. All I want to do is huddle in a corner and cry, but instead I head into the bathroom and turn the shower on. Then I lock the door and strip.

The water is warm, and I sigh in relief as I stand under the spray. Eventually, my goosebumps fade and my shivering stops. I'm still lightheaded, but I attribute that more to a lack of food than anything else.

It's hard to keep my hair from getting more wet, but I manage okay. When I turn off the water and step out of the shower, I realize I don't have anything to dry off with.

"Shit," I mutter.

I try to wipe off as much water as I can before pulling my clothes back on. Then I step back into the bedroom, immediately regretting it. The bathroom warmed up significantly from the shower, and stepping into the main room feels like I'm inside the walk-in cooler at work.

I hear someone at the door and freeze. *Not again. Not this soon.*

It opens, and the kid from earlier slips through. He looks at me in a way that, strangely, reminds me of Rhett.

I wish he was here, I think, blinking back tears.

"I can't help you escape," the kid says, twisting a blanket nervously in his hands. "Jordan would kill me. But this—I think I can get away with this."

I stare at him. He looks so young. How did he get involved in this kind of life? "How old are you?"

"Just turned nineteen last week." He tosses the blanket onto the floor next to me. "And if anyone asks, I'm not the one who gave that to you."

A deep voice calls out from downstairs. "Andrew?"

His eyes go wide. "Gotta go."

The door closes, and I hear the lock sliding back into place. I grab the blanket and wrap it around my shoulders, doing my best to ease the tightening in my chest. But it's no use.

You could've left it unlocked, I want to yell. *You could've given me a chance.*

Then I shake my head. He's just a kid—he's doing the best he can. I want out of here, but I don't want Andrew to get himself killed trying to help me, either.

They'll come for me. I know they'll come for me.

The thought is meant to soothe me, but all it does is make my eyes fill with tears again.

I know they'll find me.

That's not the question.

The question is when they'll realize they need to.

CHAPTER EIGHT

Elliot

"Got him," I say into my radio, staring down at the body from my hiding place next to the advanced trail. "Let's deal with the body and get out of here."

It doesn't take too much time. Sparrow doesn't care what happens to the body—just wanted the man dead. So we bury him a decent ways off the trail, making sure not to leave any blood behind. Someone will find him in the spring. There's no way we could get him in the ground, so he's just deep in the snow.

We're back to our cabin before nine, packing up and getting ready to leave. Unfortunately, the earliest flight opening is around midnight tonight. We're all impatient to get back home, but it's the best we can do.

There's no reason to stick around at the cabin, and I think all of us want to get to some place with cell service so we can call Wren. She's off today, and as long as she's awake, we should be able to talk to her.

We check into a hotel near the airport under the fake names we used to reserve the cabin. None of us have any desire to do any exploring around here. The fewer cameras—and people—that catch our faces, the better.

After we dump our stuff in our room, I turn my phone on and set it on the desk. It'll take a while for any messages and notifications I got to come through, so I figure I'll let it sit for a couple minutes.

Besides, we have some celebrating to do. Well, it's not *just* celebrating. Sex after a job is a way for us to release the leftover tension and stress we usually end up with.

I turn to the bed. Oliver is already sitting on the edge, a lazy grin on his face. I straddle him, tilting his head up with a finger under his chin. Instantly, his gaze turns needy, and his lips part in anticipation of a kiss. I give him what he wants, gently nipping at his bottom lip.

When we pull away, I notice that Rhett has settled into the chair in the corner. His shoulders are sagging, and his breathing is slow.

"Not joining us?" I ask.

"Happy to watch." The barest hint of a smirk flickers across his face.

"That's fine by me." I enjoy having an audience, and while it doesn't get Oliver off, he doesn't mind.

I crawl off the bed and move to my bag. After digging around for a second, I pull out lube and some ropes. When Oliver sees them, his eyes light up.

"Get up," I say.

He stands without hesitation.

After tossing the ropes onto the bed, I pull Oliver's shirt over his head. Then I take my time, leaving a trail of kisses down his neck, across his chest, and then down his stomach. Gently, I bite at the skin right by his waistband.

Oliver grunts. "I was hoping that since you have Wren to tease now, you wouldn't need to do it so much to me."

I grin at him as I yank his pants down. "Quite the opposite. Now I get to do it twice as much."

70

He rolls his eyes.

"Oh, is that what we're doing? Pretending we don't like things we actually love?" I stand, smiling slyly.

He starts to respond, but I pick him up and throw him onto the bed before he can. With a laugh, he props himself up on his elbows.

"Get up against the headboard," I say.

He obeys, settling against the pillows. I have him spread out his arms so I can tie his wrists to the headboard, double-checking that the ropes aren't too tight as I do.

"I love having you like this," I murmur, sitting back and looking at him. "I can do whatever I want to you, and you just have to take it."

He whines, and it pulls a smirk from me. I take his dick in my hand, stroking lightly. *Too* lightly. But the glare Oliver gives me is half-hearted at best. He knows I'll make it good for him. Always do.

After a minute, he starts squirming and letting out desperate noises. "Ell, please. I need you."

Moving closer, I guide my dick so it's lined up with his, taking both of them in my hand. Oliver groans as I stroke up and down. After a second, I squirt on some lube so everything slides nice and easy, and then I get back into position.

"Christ," Oliver groans. His eyes are closed, and he's resting his head against the headboard. Everything about him is . . . fucking perfect. His skin, his hair, the lines and edges and curves of his body. Completely, utterly perfect. And all mine.

"I love you."

It takes me a second to realize the words come from my mouth. I'm supposed to be teasing Oliver right now. Saying the right things that heighten the experience for both of us, not getting all sappy. But when the feelings hit, I can't really stop them. And having Oliver tied up is one of the greatest reminders that he trusts me fully.

It's important to me—knowing they all trust me. It's one of the things that should automatically come with loving someone, but I know from firsthand experience that's not always the case. And fuck, it's painful as hell.

Oliver opens his eyes slowly. His eyebrows furrow in a look of cautious worry.

Fuck. I completely ruined the moment. Goddammit.

"I love you too, Ell." He says it gently. Carefully, like I'm on the verge of tears. Shit, maybe I am.

I blow out a breath. "I'm sorry. I—"

Oliver raises an eyebrow in a challenge, making me stop. "You're sorry you love me?"

"Fuck. No, I didn't mean it like that. Ol, of course—"

He's smiling. "Shut up and kiss me, Ell."

I do, fitting my mouth to his. Now *I'm* the desperate one. All of these thoughts and feelings came out of nowhere, and I just want to get back to making Oliver feel good.

"You could never be sorry for loving me," he teases once I pull away. "I'm too cute. Wren says so."

That makes me smile. Oliver has always been the one who's able to lighten my mood with a few sentences.

He thrusts into my hand, his dick rubbing against mine in a way that makes us both groan. I move my hand up, squeezing lightly when I reach the tip of our cocks before making my way back down.

"Fuck." I kiss Oliver again. It's sloppy and unfocused because the sensations are too fucking good, but he eats it up anyway.

I set an even pace with my hand, absorbing Oliver's moans with my lips against his. I slide my tongue into his mouth, meeting his gently.

"So good, Ell," he pants.

Every noise that comes out of his mouth drives me closer to finishing. My phone goes off, but the sound barely registers in my mind.

"Come on me," Oliver says breathlessly. "Cover me with your cum. Please."

"Shit." His words send me tumbling over the edge. I have to grab his shoulder to brace myself as ropes of cum shoot out and hit his stomach.

My phone goes off again, and for a moment I'm worried that something is wrong. But the thought is so fleeting that it's gone the second it pops into my head.

"Fuck yes," Oliver says, staring down at his stomach.

I have to fight with my body to stay upright as I pull my dick from my hand and continue stroking Oliver. His balls are tight, so he's not far behind me.

"Look at me," I murmur.

He does, licking his lips in between harsh breaths. His eyes are on fire in the best way, and I savor how alive he looks in the moment. Then I pick up the pace of my hand.

"Ell," he gasps.

"Make a mess, O. Come everywhere."

"Fuck." Oliver thrusts into my hand. "Ell. Elliot!" He lets out something between a high-pitched moan and a shout. His back arches, and then he's coming all over my hand and his stomach. By the time he's finished, he's limp and panting, only held up by the restraints.

I kiss him. "Good boy."

"Goddamn," he moans.

After cleaning off my hand, I untie him and start cleaning him up with tissues. My phone goes off *again,* and the worry I felt earlier comes back tenfold.

"Jesus, Ell," Rhett says, grabbing it from the desk. "Sounds like someone's desperate to talk to you."

"Can you see if it's important?" I finish cleaning up Oliver before slipping my boxers and pants back on.

"Finn called you a couple times," Rhett replies. "And then . . ." He goes silent, tapping the screen and staring down at it. The content look on his face fades.

Noises start coming from my phone, like he's playing a video. And then I hear the unmistakable sound of Wren shouting.

"Rhett?" I say.

He doesn't respond.

Shit.

Stepping up next to him, I peer down at my phone. Then I yank it from Rhett's hands, scrolling through the messages he has pulled up.

Unknown Number: This is Jordan Williams. She'll pay for what you've done.

"What's going on?" Oliver says. He's already mostly dressed. "Please tell me that wasn't Wren's voice."

I scroll to the most recent video Jordan sent and play it.

Please still be alive. Please, love.

Watching Wren struggle for air is excruciating. And when she stops fighting while her head is still underwater, a panic I've only felt a few times before spreads through my entire body.

I feel Oliver come up beside me just as Jordan yanks Wren's head above water. "Oh my god," he murmurs.

"You're learning," Jordan says to Wren. "Now look at the camera." Once she's staring at us, her expression terrified and exhausted, Jordan shouts, "Look at her. Soaked to the bone, freezing, and half-drowned. This is what happens when you fuck with the wrong people. I hope you learn your lesson."

Wren takes a deep breath, like she knows she's about to go back under, before blurting, "I'm in a house sur-"

Her sentence is cut off by Jordan shoving her head underwater again. She doesn't fight him, just lets it happen. And when he makes no move to let her up, it becomes hard for *me* to breathe.

Hang on, Wren. Please. I'm so sorry.

"He's going to kill her," Oliver whispers. One of his hands is gripping my arm painfully, but I don't shake him off.

When Jordan finally pulls her up, I have to blink back tears of relief. But almost immediately, he forces her back under.

"No," I murmur. My free hand clenches into a fist involuntarily, my fingernails digging into my palm.

Jordan does it again. And again.

By the time he releases Wren, she looks like she can barely keep herself upright. Two men grab her and drag her out of view. My heart clenches when I lose sight of her, but at least she's still breathing.

She's still alive. We can still find her.

Jordan comes to stand in front of the camera. The smile on his face is sickening. "I'm going to find you. All of you. And once I have you here, I'm going to kill her in front of you. Slowly. Painfully. You'll learn not to mess with me."

Please be a dream. I just need to wake up. This can't be real.

The video ends. All three of us stare at my phone in silence. My throat feels clogged up, and when I manage to swallow, it aches.

It's not until Rhett speaks that it's solidified in my mind that this is very, very real.

"We're going to find her," he says lowly. "And we're not going to stop until we do."

"We can't wait until tonight." My mind is already going a mile a minute, working through all the different ways we can get back sooner. "Fuck. Give me a minute."

I pull up the number for my contact at the airport, pacing as the phone rings.

"Hey, man. What's up?"

"I need that plane off the ground in under an hour. What's your price to make it happen? A hundred thousand? Two? Three? I need to get home *now.*"

"You'd pay that much just to get back twelve hours earlier?"

"I'd sell my fucking soul if I could."

"Hey, whatever. It's your money. How about four?"

"Consider it done. We'll be there soon."

I yank a shirt over my head and grab my bag. Thankfully, we didn't really get a chance to unpack anything.

Downstairs, the girl at the counter is confused as to why we're checking out so quickly, but thankfully she doesn't ask a lot of questions.

On the way to the airport, I call Finn.

"Thank fuck," he says. "I was worried I wouldn't be able to reach you for a couple more days."

"Tell me everything you know."

"Wren called me last night, but she was gone by the time I got to the apartment. There was a bloody knife on the floor, but that was the only evidence of a break-in. The apartment complex's security cameras were wiped. I've been trying to figure out who took her, but I don't have a lot to go on."

Fuck. Did she get cut? All the videos Jordan sent were either poorly lit or at awkward angles. It's possible she has a knife wound that we couldn't see. If it gets infected . . . shit. We need to get to her *now.*

"It was Jordan Williams," I say. "He's keeping her somewhere."

"Torture?"

"Drowning."

"Shit. She's still alive?"

"For now. He wants us there when he kills her."

"Christ. Elliot, I'm so sorry."

Despite how much I'd love to blame all of this on Finn, I know that wouldn't be fair. "It's not your fault. I shouldn't've thought she'd be safe in her apartment."

My reasoning was that it's a fairly secure building. There are cameras, and on top of that, there are plenty of potential witnesses around. It's not the ideal spot to try to kidnap someone from. But apparently, Jordan is willing to be reckless. Hopefully that means he's stupid, too.

"We'll get her back," Finn says.

"Oh, there's no question about it." We'll find her. And then we'll crush every bone in that man's body for what he's done to her.

"What do you need me to do?"

"Get the info on all of the Williams' properties. I know it's a lot, but you can narrow it down to residentials. Wren said in one of the videos that she's in a house. Our plane is taking off as soon as possible, and then we'll be home. I'll have a better plan by the time we land."

"On it. You guys probably already have some type of plan to make him suffer, don't you?"

"Trust me," I say darkly. "He'll get what he deserves."

CHAPTER NINE

Wren

A week.

That's how long the guys said they might be gone for. All three of them sounded like they wanted to get back sooner, but I knew it wasn't something they could promise. And since they have no idea I'm in trouble, they have no reason to rush things.

I start pacing in my room, my blanket pulled tight around my shoulders. *A week.* Can I hold out that long? I'm honestly not sure.

Pausing in front of one of the windows, I peer outside. The snow is blinding due to the early afternoon sun, making me blink rapidly. It's been a couple hours since Andrew gave me my blanket. My hair is still damp, but at least I have something to help my body retain heat.

I need to find a way to escape.

Leaving on foot would be a stupid, dangerous move. I'd freeze. And I have no idea how close we are to civilization, or which direction to head in.

There are two cars in the driveway. If I could manage to get out of this room, find and steal the keys, and sneak into one of them without getting caught, I could have a chance. There are two men who walk the perimeter of the yard together, and they'd definitely be a problem. If I drive off, they'd probably shoot at me.

But if I can start the car and head down the driveway while they're in the back of the yard, I'll be out of view. The driveway enters the forest and turns after about twenty yards. If I can make it that far, the trees will give me some amount of cover from any bullets they send my way once they realize what's going on.

It's the only plan I can think of, and I have to admit, it's a shitty one. First of all, I can't even get out of this room. And if I manage, it'll definitely be noisy. From what I can tell, Jordan always has at least two men in the house plus him. Even if I manage to break out of here, I can't fight off that many people.

The only option I can think of is trying to convince Andrew to let me out if he comes back in alone. If he's afraid of getting killed, maybe we could run away together. That's a big if, though.

I sigh, staring at the cars. They're so close, yet they're entirely un-reachable at the same time.

The sound of the lock turning in the door fills the room, and I turn. The door flies open so hard it hits the wall and bounces back, knocking Jordan in the shoulder as he marches through.

"I'm sick of waiting. Where are they?" he demands.

"I already told you I don't know."

He advances toward me, eyes burning with fury. "This," he hisses, snatching the blanket from me. "Who gave this to you?"

I don't even skip a beat. "One of the older guys. The one with the finger tattoos."

"Don't lie to me, woman. It was Andrew, wasn't it?"

I shake my head.

"Months of training," Jordan snarls, "all wasted because you made him go soft. I knew he wasn't cut out to work for me."

Two of his men move into the room, and my stomach sinks.

"It wasn't him," I say again.

"I just told you, don't lie to me!" Jordan shouts. Then he turns to his men. "Bring her outside."

I manage a solid kick to one of their sides, but that's all I can do before they're grabbing me and dragging me downstairs. It's freezing outside, especially since I'm barely clothed and my hair is still damp. The cold air stings my skin, and the bottoms of my feet instantly ache from the cold.

They shove me onto the snowy ground while Jordan yells to two men who're circling the perimeter of the yard.

"Andrew! Get over here!"

My heart skips a beat as Andrew jogs toward us. Once he's closer, he spots the blanket in Jordan's hand, and his expression fades into one of worry and fear.

"Tell me, Andrew," Jordan drawls, "what are rules for?"

"Uh . . . for—"

"To keep things in order," Jordan shouts.

"Right. Sorry, sir."

"You know what happens when things get *out* of order?"

Andrew shakes his head, gulping. His gaze flits to me for a split second before he looks back to Jordan.

"Everything goes wrong, that's what. I had her in there with nothing to keep her warm for a *reason!* They need to know she was miserable. They need to suffer the way I have, knowing my brother was taken far too soon."

"She had nothing to do with Tyler's death," Andrew argues.

That's not exactly true.

"But her men did. And the best way to hurt them is to hurt her."

Andrew hesitates, obviously uncomfortable. But then he sighs. "I'm sorry, sir. It won't happen again."

"Damn right it won't," Jordan says before drawing his gun.

"No," I shout, lunging forward. His men pull me back with too much force, and I slip in the snow before they yank me upright again. "Don't kill him. Please."

Andrew's eyes are wide. He backs away, shaking his head. "My little brother. He needs me. I'm the only family he's got left."

"Maybe you should've thought of that before disobeying a direct order."

"I'm sorry," Andrew says. Tears spill onto his cheeks. "I promise I'll do better. Just don't take me away from him. He doesn't have anyone else."

"On your knees," Jordan says, raising his gun.

Andrew hesitates, but then he does as he's told. I close my eyes, fighting tears of my own. This can't be happening. How could Jordan kill him over this? Over a fucking *blanket?*

"Open your eyes, Wren."

I stare at the ground.

"Look at him!"

I keep my head bowed. There's no way I can watch this.

Too young. He's too young to die like this.

Just then, I hear the crunch of snow and gravel under tires. I look up, watching as a sleek black car pulls up the drive. It's caught Jordan's attention, too, and he turns to face it, his gun hanging at his side.

Hope ignites in my heart despite the cold seeping into my bones. Could it be them? Did they find out what happened somehow?

The car stops mere feet away from Jordan. The driver's side door opens, and a man steps out. When he turns to face us, my blood runs cold, and the hope in my chest is instantly snuffed out.

Jordan was right.

Black boots. Dark pants. And that red leather jacket.

Ludo Holloway.

"I've been waiting for you to show up," Jordan says.

"I'm sure," Ludo drawls, taking in the scene. His gaze runs over Andrew with an almost amused disinterest, but when he sees me, he raises an eyebrow. "What's going on here?"

I shift, all of a sudden feeling too exposed. But Jordan's men are holding my arms too tightly. I can't try to cover myself up.

"None of your business," Jordan snaps. "What do you want?"

Ludo's eyes are still trained on me as he says, "Well, I *was* going to offer you a partnership of sorts. But not anymore."

"What, am I not good enough for you all of a sudden?" Jordan's voice is mocking, but I don't miss the hint of insecurity in it, and I highly doubt Ludo does either.

"I don't make a habit of entering into deals with dead men walking." Ludo finally breaks my gaze, nodding toward Andrew. "You have no idea who he is, do you?"

"What the hell are you talking about?"

Ignoring Jordan, Ludo says, "Get in the car, boy. You're coming with me."

"You'll do no such thing." Jordan raises his gun, aiming for Andrew, but Ludo just laughs.

What the hell is going on?

"You really want to go up against me, Williams?"

Jordan shrugs. "You're the one who came out here by yourself. Where are your bodyguards, hmm? I could kill you right where you stand. It'd certainly make my life a whole lot easier."

"My bodyguards," Ludo says with annoyance, "are in the trees with sniper rifles, waiting for you to fuck up so they can end your miserable existence."

Jordan stills. Then he glances around, looking into the snowy forest while he lowers his gun.

"You didn't actually believe that I came here alone, did you?" Ludo clicks his tongue. "So naïve. And you'll never get the chance to learn."

"What do you mean?" Jordan demands.

Andrew starts inching toward the car. Our eyes lock for a split second, and something like remorse flits across his features. But there's nothing he can do to help me—he's as powerless as I am.

Ludo ushers Andrew toward the car, turning his back on Jordan. It's a bold move considering the man is holding a gun. An act of mockery, even.

Just as Ludo is about to get into the driver's seat, he gives Jordan a pitying smile. "Here I thought I'd have to manipulate you out of your power. Or take it from you by force. But you won't even be alive by the end of the week. Good day, Jordan. Enjoy it. It might be your last."

Is he going to leave me here?

"Wait," I call out.

But Ludo ignores me, getting in and slamming his door.

"No," I whisper as he drives off.

I can barely make out Andrew's stricken expression through the back window. And then Jordan's body is blocking my view. He crouches in front of me, his face contorted with rage.

"This," he grits out, "is your fault."

It's not. I know it. Jordan knows it. But none of that matters. I'm going to pay anyway.

This time, in the cold and damp cellar, I don't fight at all. I focus on holding my breath, on telling myself that I can make it until he pulls me from the water. I let myself believe that I'll find a way to escape, even though it feels like I'm going to die down here.

And when Jordan's men lock me away upstairs, I crawl into the bathroom and sit in the tub while the shower warms me up. It helps me feel a little better, but my stomach still aches from a lack of food.

By the time I've tried to dry off and taken a few sips of water from the sink, I'm exhausted. But I don't let myself sleep. If a chance for me to escape—however slim—presents itself, I have to be ready to take it.

So I wait.

And wait.

And wait some more.

CHAPTER TEN

Rhett

I can't stop watching the videos.

What's worse, Elliot receives another one after we land.

I'm not sure whether I should be relieved or concerned that Wren wasn't fighting in this one. Is it because she's given up hope? Or because she's trying to conserve her energy? Either way, we need to get to her *now*.

"Just let her go," Elliot says. "Do what you want to us, but leave her out of this."

This is his third time calling Jordan and the first time the asshole decided to pick up. From the expression on Elliot's face, the conversation isn't going well.

Once our plane landed, Elliot and I came directly home. Oliver said he had to check on something and that he'd follow us soon. He wouldn't tell us where he was going, and I'm not gonna lie, it pissed me off. But he promised he'd be back soon.

As for me, I've been doing a couple things. The first is sorting through the residential properties that the Williams family owns. Finn emailed them to Elliot before we even landed, which is way sooner than I was expecting. That's what happens when you're friends with powerful people.

In the videos, Wren was in what appeared to be a cellar of some sort. The way it was built looks like it was an older house, so I'm sorting out newer ones. And I'm also flagging the ones that are in less-populated areas. The more secluded a place is, the better a hiding spot it is.

The second thing I've been up to is learning more about Jordan. More specifically, his girlfriend. I'd never hurt her—she's just as innocent in all of this as Wren is—but Jordan doesn't know that.

"Jordan, please."

I sigh, watching Elliot pace the length of his office. It's been years since we've felt this helpless, and the strain in Ell's voice tells me he's as ready to rip Jordan's head off as I am.

"Give me the phone," I say quietly.

Elliot shakes his head, glancing at my laptop screen. No doubt, he knows exactly what I've been up to. "Then what do you want, Jordan? You want us to turn ourselves over?" A pause, and then, "No, Jordan, don't—goddammit."

My anger only spikes when Elliot slides his phone into his pocket.

"He hung up on you?"

Ell nods. "He said that because we made him wait, he's going to make us wait. And that he won't exchange us for her. He won't stop until all four of us are dead."

"So we threaten him before he can hurt Wren anymore. All we have to do is send proof that we have the means to kill his girlfriend. I have her address pulled up right here."

Elliot throws his hands up in exasperation. "And if he decides to re-taliate by doing something worse to Wren? What then, Rhett? Christ."

"We have to do *something*."

"We have to be careful," Elliot says. "Jordan wants revenge. This isn't your typical hostage situation. He's not going to give her back in exchange for something. He's trying to lure us into a trap to kill us all. Although right now he's unnecessarily drawing things out."

"Right now, all he's doing is *hurting her*," I shout. "We have to find her, Ell."

"I know," he says gently. "We will."

"But we *aren't*," I grit out. "We're just sitting here. Doing fucking nothing."

"No, we're not." He points to my laptop. "You've gone through the properties?"

"Yes, but—"

"Which ones fit our criteria?"

With a grumble, I pull up the three properties I've marked as the ones Jordan is most likely to be hiding Wren at. They're all in different directions. If splitting up was an option, it wouldn't be a problem. But Jordan has a lot of resources at his fingertips. There's no way he won't be guarding the house. Splitting up could be a deadly mistake.

"We start with this one," Elliot says, pointing to a house that looks like it's in the middle of a vineyard. "You get the equipment. I'll memorize the layout of the house and get Wren a change of warmer clothes. Oh, and can you find Oliver?"

"On it." I'm already halfway out the door when Elliot stops me.

"Rhett. We can't just storm the house. We'll have to take out everyone who's not inside. And then we'll need to enter and find her strategically."

My hands curl into fists. I told Wren I'd burn the world down to find her if I ever needed to, and I fucking meant it. But everything Elliot is saying makes sense. I hate it, but he's right—about Jordan's girlfriend, about how we should get her from the house, and about most things in general.

This is a time to exercise caution. The last thing we want is Wren getting caught in the crossfire. And if we barge into the house unprepared, we could get killed before we can get to her.

"I won't do anything rash," I say, walking back over to him. I press my lips to his in a short yet reassuring kiss. "I promise."

With a sigh of relief, he runs his hands down my arms, like he needs the split second of touch to stabilize him. "Thank you."

With that, we head our separate ways. I call Oliver, but he doesn't answer. When I check the garage, his car is still gone.

I try calling him again, and then again after a few minutes.

Nothing.

Fuck.

Worst-case scenarios run through my head as I load up Elliot's SUV. By the time I'm done, I've worked myself back into some of my worst memories.

Me peering through a crack in a door, watching Oliver as he claimed to be working alone. The gun pointed at his head. The utter helplessness that almost overwhelmed me in the moment.

Not again. I can't go through that again.

But apparently, my thoughts aren't enough to keep reality from crashing in. My phone vibrates in my pocket. As I read the text, my blood runs cold.

"Ell," I shout, my eyes still glued to my screen. And then I'm running through the house, trying to get to him faster.

Because we can't waste a single second.

CHAPTER ELEVEN

Oliver

The drive from the airport to Evolve is only fifteen minutes, but it feels like an hour. I'm operating on a hunch, but if Ludo knows where Wren is—and I bet he does—then he might be our best bet to getting to her the fastest. The thought doesn't do anything to soothe the anger expanding in my chest, though. Because if he knows where she is, then why the fuck hasn't he given us a heads up yet?

By the time I've parked, I've imagined ten different ways to wring the information out of Ludo if he doesn't volunteer it easily. I can't do any of them—I'm not stupid—but I can at least pretend.

When I shove the doors to the club open, I come face to face with a large man dressed in all black.

"Sir, the club doesn't open until much later tonight. Only staff members are allowed inside right now."

"Where's Holloway?" I snap, brushing past him.

"You can't just barge in here—"

"Really? Because it sure looks like I did."

"Sir, I'm going to have to ask you—"

"Holloway," I shout. "You get your ass down here right *fucking* now."

"Already here," a deep voice drawls from somewhere to my left. "Just enjoying the show."

I whip around just as the guard grabs me. He tries to drag me back toward the entrance, but I shove him off me.

"Where is she?" I demand.

"Who?"

"Wren! Do you know where Jordan is keeping her? Because I swear to god, Ludo, if I find out you know where she is and you're doing *nothing,* I'll—"

"Careful, Oliver. Are you really about to say you'd kill the most powerful man in Philadelphia on camera?" Ludo gestures upward toward the security cameras. "Doesn't sound like a smart move to me."

"Do you know where he has her?" I grit out.

"Jordan. Jordan Williams?"

I nod.

Ludo shrugs. "Why would I? It's not like we're business partners or anything."

"I saw the way you were watching Wren last weekend. Tell me you haven't been keeping tabs on her. Go ahead. Lie to my face."

With a sigh, Ludo slips his hands into the pockets of his red leather jacket. "I may be known as a lot of things, Moore. Ruthless, cruel, brilliant. But one thing you need to understand is that when I see a line, I think long and hard before I cross it. You following?"

"She's ours."

"Exactly. And I quite like having the three of you as my allies, regardless of whether your woman is my type or not. I haven't touched her, I don't plan on touching her, and I don't know where she is."

I'm not sure if I believe him, but I have no leverage to force an answer out of him. And, for now, we need to stay on Ludo's good side. So I move to leave, but his voice stops me.

"Do you know what he wants?"

"Revenge." I turn around again to look at him. "He figured out you ordered the kill on Edgar, but he's too scared to come after you, so he took her instead. Or at least that's our working theory."

Ludo shrugs. "I'm sure he won't kill her until he has you all there to watch."

I can't wait to rip you to shreds, you fucking monster.

"You know, if you're so desperate to get to her, why don't you get yourself kidnapped?"

"What?"

"If Jordan wants revenge, he's probably got eyes on you at all times. It's not like he doesn't have the resources, what with inheriting every-thing from his uncle. So put yourself in a vulnerable position. Get your-self kidnapped. He'll take you to wherever he's keeping Wren. I'm sure your other lovers would find a way to save you both."

"Rhett and Elliot would never go for that."

Ludo rolls his eyes. "You three and your loyalty. So what? Do you want your girl back or not? You know the phrase—ask for forgiveness, not permission."

With a parting nod, Ludo walks deeper into the club, whistling an eerie tune as he does. The guard reaches out for me again, but I slap his hand away.

"I'm going," I grouse. "I'm going."

. . .

If I make it out of this alive, Rhett and Ell are going to kill me.

Ludo fucking Holloway is the last person I ever thought I'd take advice from. But we're running out of options. Jordan is holding her underwater longer each time. And considering how out of it she looked at the end of that last video, she won't be able to make it much longer.

We're coming, princess. I promise.

Back home, I pause in front of the closed door to Elliot's office. I need to make sure they're both distracted before I leave.

"He hung up on you?" Rhett says.

"He said that because we made him wait, he's going to make us wait," Elliot replies. "And that he won't exchange us for her. He won't stop until all four of us are dead."

Fuck.

Rhett says something back, but I'm already moving away from the office. I head downstairs silently, pulling a bracelet out of my pocket and slipping it onto my wrist. It's been a while since I've worn it—haven't needed to—but it'll work perfectly for this.

I stare at the black skull charm surrounded by black beads. Inside the skull is a GPS tracking device. It was something I got years back after a job went wrong and I almost got killed. Rhett and Elliot always being able to find me seemed to ease their worries, so I wore it all the time until we got better at what we do.

Now it's the way they'll be able to find me and Wren. I'd let them in on my plan, but they'd stop me, and we're running out of time. Rhett is ready to start going after people Jordan cares about, and I can't let him do that. Not when we don't know what Jordan will do to Wren in return.

As I head to my car, I schedule a text to go out to both Rhett and Elliot, explaining where I went. By the time they'll get it, I'll be far away enough that they won't be able to stop me.

It feels like a betrayal. I'm going to be scaring the shit out of both of them, but Ludo is right. My guess is that Jordan has had people keeping an eye on our house ever since he got his hands on Wren. So if I can get myself into a vulnerable enough position, his men will probably come for me.

The whole situation makes me think that Jordan's timing is terribly off. Why kidnap her the night we left? Had he not realized yet that we were gone? Or did he do it on purpose to draw out Wren's suffering?

Regardless, the whole plan seems stupid. It would've made more sense to get us all at once. Or at least all closer together. Jordan must not fully understand who he's dealing with. Because now that we know Wren is in trouble, we'll stop at nothing to get her back.

Rhett calls me multiple times while I'm driving, but I ignore him. I can't explain anything until I'm far enough away. If they try to stop me, then this was all a waste of time.

I leave my car near an empty park. There's plenty of snow for sledding and playing outside, but it's too cold for most kids, so the place is deserted.

Before I get far, I feel my phone vibrating in my pocket. I pull it out and see Elliot's face lit up on the screen. It's past the time that I scheduled his text for, so he's definitely read it. Guilt twists in my chest, but I don't turn back. The park is a good place to catch me alone and off guard.

"I'm sorry," I say when I take the call.

"Why are you doing this?"

The anguish in Elliot's voice has my heart aching in a way I promised myself I'd never have to experience again. I close my eyes against the pain, but it doesn't help at all.

"Why, Oliver?" he asks again.

The answer to his question is one I've been grappling with for a couple days. Ever since we took Wren to Evolve, really. It feels too fast, but I can't deny the way I feel, even if it sounds naïve or rash.

"Because I love her, Ell."

For a suffocatingly long time, there's silence on the other end of the line. Then Elliot sighs. "I know."

"She needs us. You saw her in that last video. One of these times, Jordan is going to keep her under for too long, and she's not gonna be able to hold out for long enough."

"And what about what Jordan will do to *you?* What if he decides to kill *you?* Please don't do this. We can find another—"

"I'm not waiting any longer."

"O, you *just* got back on your meds. You can't—"

"Then I guess you'd better come get me before it's time to take my next pill."

"Oliver!" His voice breaks in the telltale way that means he's close to tears. And fuck, I haven't seen Elliot cry in a long time.

"I'll be okay," I say gently.

"You don't know that," he pleads. "You did this without any planning, and you're by yourself, and what if the bracelet falls off or they take it away or the tracker stops working, and—"

"Ell, it'll all work out."

"Why does it have to be you?" he shouts.

"You never would've gone for this. And I don't want Wren to have to be alone. Just get us out as soon as you can."

"What if we can't find you?" he whispers.

"You will. I trust you."

"Oliver . . ." The terrified desperation in his voice has tears pricking in my own eyes.

"I love you," I manage. "Please tell Rhett I love him, too."

"Ol-"

I hang up and shove my phone in my pocket. This is the right thing to do. We need to get to Wren as quickly as we possibly can, and if Rhett and Elliot follow closely enough, they could rescue me and Wren within a matter of hours.

That's what I try to tell myself, anyway. But Elliot's distressed voice echoes in my mind, and even though I'm doing this for Wren, I can't help but hate myself a little for how this will affect Elliot and Rhett. There's no doubt that this is bringing up memories we'd all rather forget about.

I'm so lost in thought that when I feel the cold barrel of a gun pressing against the back of my head, I actually *am* taken off guard.

"Get on your knees," a gruff voice says from behind me.

Slowly, I do, raising my hands in surrender.

He huffs. "You're a fucking idiot, you know that?"

I laugh. "Yeah. Yeah, I know."

CHAPTER TWELVE

Wren

The house is oddly quiet. A couple hours ago, I watched Jordan and two of his men pile into a car and leave. It has me wondering how many people are even here right now. I've been trying to keep track of the different voices I hear, and I'm pretty sure there's only one man in the house—especially since I haven't heard any type of conversation since Jordan left.

I'm still trapped in this stupid room, but with the element of surprise on my side, maybe I could manage to get the hell out of here. That is, *if* someone decides to check on me. Trying to break down the door would make too much noise, and whoever's in the house would know exactly what's going on.

But still, this is the best chance I have at escaping. I have to try something.

What would Elliot do?

Oliver has said on multiple occasions that I remind him of Elliot. He's the thinker. The planner. The one who figures out the best way to navigate any type of situation, like a chess player who's always thinking ten moves ahead.

I can do that, too. And I can find the strength—mental and physical—to make it out of this alive. I have to.

So I go through the bathroom, looking for anything that I could use as a weapon. But the cabinet under the sink is empty. All I have is a bar of fucking soap.

As I'm about to turn away, I realize that's not true. The lid to the top of the toilet could do a decent amount of damage if I'm able to get close enough to someone. Which I potentially could if I can keep the element of surprise.

Quietly, I take the lid off. It's porcelain, so it's kind of heavy, but that's a good thing in this case. Then I tiptoe to the door, gripping the lid tightly.

As long as I can get out of this room, I think I have a decent chance of escaping. There's still a car in the driveway, so all I have to do is find the keys for it. From there, I'll need to wait until the two men who are walking the perimeter of the yard are behind the house. They won't see me heading down the driveway, and then I should be clear.

I'm not sure where to go from there, but I'll figure it out. It can't take long until I hit a main road, right?

You can do this, Wren. One step at a time.

"Help," I yell. "Help me, please!"

Pausing, I listen for movement downstairs. It takes a second, but then the sound of footsteps on the stairs reaches me.

Perfect.

"Help," I shout again, adding in as much fear and desperation to my voice as I can.

When I hear the door unlocking, my stomach jumps. But I steady myself, raising the lid over my head so I'm ready to strike.

The door opens, and when one of Jordan's men steps through, I slam the lid over his head. He stumbles, but it isn't enough force to knock him out. With a yell, he lunges toward me, knocking the lid out of my hands. I manage to knee him in the balls, which causes him to double over, and then I slam my elbow into his back.

He falls to his knees, momentarily disoriented. It gives me just enough time to grab the lid again and whack him on the head. This time, he crumples to the floor with a *thud*, unconscious.

I don't waste any time. First, I search his pockets, and relief spreads through my chest when I find what looks like a set of car keys. Then I grab his gun, keeping it in my hands so I can use it at a moment's notice.

Outside the room, I lock the door hastily so he can't come after me. The house is quiet, but I still sneak down the stairs. The first floor is fairly open, and thankfully I don't see anyone else.

So far, so good.

Silently, I creep to one of the windows, peering out. The two guys walking the perimeter still have the driveway in their view, but only for another minute or so. And once the car is out of their sight, I'll have a very short time frame to get into it and down the driveway. There won't be a second to waste.

I'd kill them, but I've never actually shot a gun before. What if my aim is off and all I do is attract attention to myself? No, the best option is to try to get away without them noticing.

Once the house is almost blocking their view, I head outside through the front door. It's freezing, and I realize I should've looked for a coat or at least taken the shirt from the man I knocked out. But I don't have time to turn back.

Once I'm in the car, I shut the door quietly and turn it on, praying that the engine turning over isn't loud enough to attract attention. And then I head down the driveway as fast as I can considering it's covered in snow.

It's surrounded by trees on either side, and there's a turn before it hits the road. Just as I finish following the curve, I slam on the brakes. An SUV is heading up the driveway.

The car slides a bit before coming to a full stop. There's no way for me to even try to get around the SUV. The trees make it too tight. So I get out, diving into the trees. It's just starting to get dark out, but it's not enough to conceal me.

A car door slams behind me. I don't even make it thirty seconds before a large body is tackling me to the ground. The snow helps to cushion my fall, but it still hurts.

"No," I scream as two pairs of hands yank me up. I try to twist out of their grasp, but it's me against two men. They take me back to the SUV, lifting me and throwing me into the trunk.

As the door slams shut, I scramble to my hands and knees, only to come face to face with Oliver. His hands are zip tied behind his back, and he has a cut on his cheek.

What?

"Hey, princess." He gives me a half-hearted smile.

"No. No, no no *no*. Oliver, how—"

"Shh," he soothes. "I need you to calm down. Deep breaths, Wren."

I shake my head as tears fill my eyes. Gently, I brush over the cut on his cheek. What happened? How did they kidnap Oliver, too? And if he's here, then where are Elliot and Rhett?

The SUV lurches forward. Carefully, I peer into the front of the vehicle. There's one man driving, and Jordan is in the passenger seat. The other man who got me into the trunk is currently driving the car I stole.

"I was so close," I whisper.

"I know, princess. I'm sorry."

"Oliver, I can't go back. I can't do it again. He's going to kill me." It's a struggle to keep my voice down, but somehow I barely manage.

"Listen to me," he says quietly. "You're going to be okay. But don't agitate him more. Just let them bring us inside."

"Oliver, no—"

"Yes, Wren. Trust me."

I look into his eyes, trying to figure out what he means—what he knows but can't say. But the only thing I see is fear.

"Please," he whispers as the SUV comes to a stop in front of the house. I nod. "Okay."

The trunk door opens, and Jordan's men pull both of us out. I cringe against the cold, but they don't keep us outside for long. Every part of me wants to fight against the man holding me, but I follow Oliver's lead. He's walking calmly, letting two men shove him around as they bring us through the house.

Jordan follows us upstairs, where we can hear a pounding of sorts.

"Let me out! Get me out of here!"

The man I fought earlier must be awake. *Shit.* I wasn't supposed to be here when they discovered him.

Jordan unlocks the door and throws it open. "Seriously?" he yells. "How the hell did she get the better of you?"

"She surprised me," the guy says, staring at the ground in embarrassment. His head is bloody from where I hit him.

Jordan turns to me, and his eyes are void of everything except hate. "You thought you could get away?" He advances toward me until he's in my face. "You thought you could outsmart me? Stupid girl."

"Fuck you," I grit out.

My defiance earns me a slap to the face, which makes Oliver try to fight against the men holding him. My cheek stings, but I don't care. If

Oliver is back, that means Elliot and Rhett are home, too. Beforehand, I was beginning to lose hope. But with Oliver here, it's like I have access to some secret reserve of strength that's deep within me.

I'm still scared as hell. And if I find myself in that cellar again, I'm not sure I'll make it out alive. But I just need to not think about that. Elliot and Rhett will find us. I know they will.

"No one comes in here by themselves," Jordan yells, snatching the toilet lid from the ground. "Lock them up. And I want two of you guarding the door at all times."

The men release us, shoving Oliver to his knees before exiting the room. The second the lock slides into place, I run to him. Crouching down, I throw my arms around him. He's warm and familiar and safe. A little piece of home in this hellish nightmare.

"Shit, Wren. You're freezing."

"I'll be okay."

"No—fuck. Let me get up."

I help him to his feet. Carefully, he bends at his knees and brings his hands down. Then he steps through his arms so his hands are in front of him. "Can you tighten the zip tie for me?"

"What? *Tighten* it?"

"Trust me, princess." He holds his hands out to me. Once I've tightened the zip tie as much as I can, he steps back from me and raises his hands above his head. Then, with his elbows open, he brings his arms down hard until they connect with his sides. The force breaks the plastic, and it falls to the ground.

My eyes widen. "I didn't know you could do that."

"I'll teach you how to do it once we're out of here," he says as he pulls his T-shirt over his head. "Here. Put this on."

I do. It smells like him, vanilla with a hint of woodiness. Despite our situation, it helps me to relax.

"C'mere, princess." Oliver opens his arms to me, and I step into them immediately, burying my face in his neck. He holds me so tightly I'm afraid he might squeeze the life right out of me, but I don't mind. All I want is to be as close to him as possible.

"How did they kidnap you?" I ask.

"I let them on purpose," he says quietly.

"What?!" I try to pull away, but he refuses to let me out of his arms.

"Shh, keep your voice down, princess. Is the room bugged?"

"I—I don't know."

Looking around, he says, "I highly doubt it is, but just in case . . ." He takes my hand and pulls me into the bathroom. After he turns on the shower, he raises his wrist. "See this bracelet?"

I nod.

"It has a GPS tracker in it. Rhett and Elliot should be on their way to us right now. They're going to get us out. And then we'll get you home."

"They let you do that?"

Oliver grimaces. "I may have told them my plan when I was already far enough away that they couldn't stop me."

"Oh my god. Oliver, they're going to be so upset."

"They are. But once we're all safe, they'll understand. It was the quickest way we could get to you. Jordan was refusing to tell us anything."

I shake my head. "Oliver, he could *kill* you."

"I'll be okay."

"No! Oliver, why? Why would you do this? If you die—"

He places a finger over my lips to quiet me. And once I've stopped talking, he rests his forehead against mine. "Because I love you, Wren.

Maybe it's too fast, but I don't care. I love you, and I'd die a thousand deaths if it meant you got out of here alive."

He loves me. The thought makes my head spin, even as my heart beats a little stronger and my breaths come a little easier. But I shake my head. "No, you can't die. What about Elliot? What about Rhett? Oliver, you can't do that to them!"

"I'm not," he says gently. "We're going to make it out of this alive, princess. All of us. Now tell me, how did you get away?"

The abrupt change of subject is mildly disorienting, but if he doesn't want to talk about this, fine. Hopefully we'll get a chance to later.

"My elbows and knees."

"What?"

"Elbows and knees. They're my best assets."

With a smirk, Oliver pulls away, his gaze running down my body. "Oh, I don't know about that, princess."

I roll my eyes. "You know what I mean. I surprised him, and then I hit him in the head with the top of the toilet, but I didn't use enough force and he knocked it out of my hands. So I used a knee here, an elbow there, knocked him out, and then ran."

Oliver snorts. "Remind me to stay on your good side."

I laugh. It's not wholehearted, but I think it's the first time I've smiled since I opened the gift they got me.

How was that only yesterday?

Oliver must sense my lingering distress. He wraps his arms around my waist, pulling me into him. "We're going to be okay, princess. They'll come for us. And between Elliot's planning skills and Rhett's anger, there's no way they won't succeed."

I find myself relaxing a little more. "You're sure?" *I can't watch you die.*

"Positive," he whispers. "I promise."

Chapter Thirteen

Elliot

Because I love her.

When the words spilled through my phone, I wasn't even surprised. Oliver fell for me and Rhett first, so it makes sense that he'd be the first to realize how deep his feelings are for Wren.

It doesn't help the hurt, though. Or the panic.

What if his plan doesn't work?

What if we lose them both?

"Ell."

I look up from my phone. Rhett is dressed and ready to go, boots already on and everything.

"We need to get moving," he says.

"Right."

Again, I stare down at my phone, tracking the blinking blue dot that's currently my only connection to Oliver. I texted him after our call, but he didn't answer, which means things are probably going according to plan. *For now.*

"Everything's in the SUV."

The blue dot blurs. Then the whole screen.

"Fuck. Ell . . ."

I try to blink my tears back, but they end up falling. Gently, Rhett takes my phone from my hand and sets it on the counter. Then he steps in front of me, resting his forehead against mine.

He doesn't say anything. But with Rhett, I don't expect him to—don't need him to. He places me firmly against his body, holding me tightly, and squeezes his eyes shut.

Get it together, Ell. You have to stay strong. For them.

"Just tell me we'll get them home safe."

"We will." Rhett says it with such confidence that it's hard not to believe him. "Now let's get moving. I want them home tonight."

He guides me through the house with his hand in mine. I can't stop staring at the blinking blue dot on my phone, like knowing exactly where Oliver is will somehow make this all better.

It doesn't.

"What if we can't—"

"Don't think like that, Ell," Rhett says as he opens the passenger side door to my SUV. Then he pushes me inside. "I need you on top of your game today. So do O and Wren."

"Right," I mumble, pulling at my seatbelt.

We drive in silence. Judging how many miles we are from Oliver, they're about forty-five minutes ahead of us. The roads aren't good enough to try going over the speed limit even with four-wheel drive. If the way Rhett is tapping the steering wheel with his fingers is any indication, it's frustrating him as much as it is me.

"They're not heading in the direction of the vineyard house," I say. "It's one of the others—probably the old one that's in the forest."

"It'll be okay," Rhett replies. "Just tell me where to go."

I direct him carefully, making sure to give him the quickest route. Then I sink into my seat as an odd mix of panic and self-doubt settles over me. Not only did we almost waste hours going to the wrong place, but I memorized the layout of the wrong damn building.

"Rhett, what if—"

"*Stop.*"

"No! What are we going to do if we're too late? If Jordan decides that killing Wren in front of Oliver is enough? What if they're both dead?"

"Then we'll make Jordan's life just as miserable as we're going to make Ludo's," he grits out. "But I need you to not catastrophize right now. Tell me what our plan is."

I take a deep breath. He's right—I need to stay focused. "Once Oliver's marker stops moving, we'll be able to identify which house he's at. We'll park the SUV nearby but out of sight. Somehow we'll have to sneak onto the property and assess what their outdoor security is. Considering Jordan thinks we have no idea where he is, it'll probably be pretty lax."

"Okay. So we neutralize any guards outside. Then what?"

"We get into the house. By then, there's a high chance that we'll have lost our element of surprise, so we'll need to be careful. Take cover whenever possible, watch each other's backs, and eliminate any threats."

"And then?"

"And then we find Oliver and Wren." Closing my eyes, I will them to be okay. "We find them and we bring them home."

"You don't sound very confident." His voice is just barely laced with worry, and I know why. I'm always confident.

"I picked the wrong house," I murmur.

"What?"

"I was going to have us go to the wrong house. What if we'd done that? How much time would we have lost?"

"Ell." His voice is gentle as he places a comforting hand on my leg. "You did the best you could with the limited information you had."

I nod, forcing myself to breathe. Oliver's plan may be all kinds of reckless and dangerous, but I understand his reasoning. It's getting us to Wren way faster than any plan I could've come up with. I'm terrified for him, and I'm hurt that he went behind our backs, but I'm grateful, too.

When Oliver's dot stops moving an eighth of a mile off the road, I double-check that it's one of the addresses that Finn sent us. Now that we have a set location that we're heading to, Rhett starts driving faster. It's not a lot—ending up in a ditch is the last thing we need right now—but it's still something. By the time we're pulling off the road and grabbing our weapons, the sun has disappeared beneath the horizon.

The darkness and the trees give us some cover as we sneak through the woods. When we come up on the house, I'm honestly surprised by the lack of guards outside. All I can see are two men walking the perimeter of the property where the snowy lawn meets the trees.

"That's it?" I mutter. It feels too easy.

For another couple minutes, we watch, making sure they're the only two outside. There could be guards hiding in the woods, but considering how smug Jordan sounded earlier, I'm pretty sure he thinks he's safe.

Not for much longer.

I kneel in the snow with my rifle, adding the silencer. Then I set my elbow on my knee for stability. "I'll take them out. Let me know if you see any movement in the trees or anywhere else."

"Got it."

I drop the men with one shot each, and then I use the night vision scope to check the woods for any potential threats.

Nothing.

"Jesus," I whisper. "I knew there was a reason Edgar picked Tyler as his heir instead of Jordan, but I didn't think he was *this* stupid."

Rhett makes a low noise of agreement before turning to me. "Ready?"

"Absolutely. Let's get this bitch."

CHAPTER FOURTEEN

Oliver

As I hold Wren in the bathroom, I let myself focus on the sliver of relief I'm feeling. I got her to laugh. If I can make her feel even a little better, that has to count for something, right? I'll take my wins where I can get them right now.

"I want to kill him," she whispers eventually.

"Who?"

"Jordan. I want to kill him, Oliver." She pulls away and looks me in the eye. "For what he's done. He almost killed a nineteen-year-old kid this morning just because he brought me a blanket. And Jordan's been so cruel. Every time he holds me underwater, I'm afraid I won't be able to hold my breath for long enough. I almost inhaled last time, Oliver. I almost tried to *inhale water* because the urge to breathe was so strong that it made more sense to me than holding my breath."

I swallow hard. If I could promise her that it won't happen again, I would. But that's not a promise I can keep. I have no idea how far behind Elliot and Rhett are. And Jordan sounded pretty damn angry when he locked us in here. If he decides to retaliate because Wren tried to escape . . .

Fuck.

"You can do it," I say, placing my hands on your shoulders. "If it happens again, just remember that he won't kill you until he has Elliot and Rhett here. And that's not gonna happen."

I absolutely hate myself for repeating Ludo's words to her. They made me see red in the moment, but right now, they're the only thing I can tell Wren to give her hope to make it through this.

"But what if Jordan thinks I can hold my breath for longer than I actually can?" she whispers.

"Let's just hope that Ell and Rhett get here soon, okay?"

She nods, sniffling. "I'm trying."

But then we both hear footsteps on the stairs, and I can't help but wonder if I jinxed us. Wren tenses in my arms.

"Shit," I mutter. In a matter of seconds, the sound of the door to the bedroom being unlocked reaches us.

"Oliver," she whispers. "Oliver, I can't do it again."

"Get behind me."

I don't wait for her to move, stepping in front of her. When the bathroom door opens, two men step in. They both glare at me, seemingly surprised I got out of the zip tie.

Idiots.

"Step out of the way," one of them says.

"You're not touching her."

"You really want to do this the hard way?"

I grin. "Always."

"Fine." He draws his gun. "I see no reason why I can't put a bullet in you. What do you think? Arm? Knee? Foot?"

"No," Wren says, forcing her way around me. "No. Leave him alone."

I try to push her behind me, but one of the men grabs her and yanks her away. Wren's eyes are filled with tears when she looks back at me.

"Wren, don't—" I step forward, reaching for her, but the man holding her presses his gun to her temple.

"You really want to test us right now?" he barks.

I freeze. "No. Sorry."

He doesn't remove the gun from her head as he backs out of the bathroom. In the bedroom, I see there's a third man waiting.

Fuck.

"Come out slowly," one of them says.

I do, keeping my hands up and my gaze on Wren. Her eyes are squeezed shut, and her entire body is shaking.

I'm sorry, princess. You deserve better than this.

The other two men grab my arms, and then they force us out of the room and downstairs. Just as I did when they brought us in, I absorb as much as I can—the open kitchen and living room, the hallway they take us down, the closed doors we pass, and then the stairs leading downward.

In the basement, they shove us into a smaller room that looks like a cellar. I recognize it as the scene of most of the videos Jordan sent us.

No. Goddammit, no.

They force me into a chair that's on the far side of a large trough full of water. While they secure me, Jordan zip ties Wren's hands behind her back. She sniffles from where she's kneeling in front of the trough.

Jordan waves his men away. "Leave us. I'll call for you when I'm done with them."

"Wren," I say, and when she looks at me, the terror in her eyes is like a knife twisting in my gut. "Wren, you can do this. I know you can." I try to bust out of the zip ties holding me to the chair, but it's no use.

"Shut up," Jordan snaps at me. He kneels behind Wren, his body caging her against the trough.

"Oliver," she whispers, the sound barely carrying to my ears. I can see in her expression just how hard she's fighting to stay calm. She's terrified, but she's trying to reach inside of herself to find the will to hold on for one more round.

I love you, I mouth.

Her lips part, like she's about to say something back, but then Jordan grabs her chin and wrenches it to the side. He leans forward so he can look into her eyes. "I bet you regret ever getting mixed up with these men, don't you?"

She spits in his face.

It's a stupid move, but I can't help but be proud of her. If the way she finds her strength is by acting on her hate for Jordan, then so be it.

Jordan grabs her hair, forcing her down until her head is submerged in the water. In the videos he sent Elliot, he always watched her. But now his eyes are on me, a sick grin on his face.

"This is your fault," he yells. "Yours. You killed my brother. You fucking shot him!"

I twist my wrists, trying to see how much wiggle room I have in the restraints. Not much. "Let her up. You've had her under for long enough."

"I don't think so," he says.

I jerk my arms, trying to break free, but I can't get enough momentum. "Let her up," I shout.

At this point, my only hope is that having a strong enough reaction will satisfy Jordan. If I give him what he wants, then maybe he won't drown Wren for as long. It could have the opposite effect—my distress could fuel his hatred—but I have to try something.

"Please, Jordan," I beg.

He yanks Wren up by her hair. Water streams down her body, soaking her clothes while she gulps in air. And while she's mid-breath, Jordan shoves her underwater again.

"No," I yell, still struggling against my restraints. "Stop!"

"If you didn't want this to happen, then you shouldn't've murdered my brother," Jordan replies. When Wren tries to lift her head out of the water, he shoves her down harder. "I told you three that you'd pay. This is only the beginning."

"You're going to burn in hell for this," I growl, and fuck, I don't even *believe* in hell.

When Jordan lets Wren up, she can't stop coughing, and the breaths she manages are short. The amount of time he held her under for was concerning. I'm panicking, and I know that has to be affecting my judgment, but I'm pretty sure he's going for longer than he did in the videos.

"Wren," I say. "Wren, I'm so—"

Jordan doesn't let her hear the rest of my sentence. He pushes her under again, slamming an elbow into her back when she starts struggling.

I've been trying to get out of these restraints, but all I've managed to do is scrape my wrists raw against the zip ties. There's nothing I can do to stop Jordan, and for the first time today, I realize that maybe this plan *was* stupid.

What if they can't get here in time?

"Jordan, please," I say. "Please don't kill her."

A sadistic smile twists his mouth. "Maybe I should. Once I have the other two, I can just kill you in front of them."

"No," I shout.

Wren isn't struggling anymore, and my only hope is that it's because she's trying to conserve energy. *Just hold on a little longer, princess.*

"She doesn't deserve this. Let her up," I beg.

Jordan's eyes flash. "Tyler didn't deserve—"

The door flies open. Elliot and Rhett barge into the room, and tears of relief fill my eyes.

Rhett grabs Jordan and yanks him off Wren. She slips to the floor, the tub obstructing her from my view, but I can hear her coughs and gasps.

She's alive. She's breathing. She'll be okay.

Rhett throws Jordan to the ground and kicks him in the face. Then he rushes to Wren, dropping to his knees and trying to pull her into a sitting position. "Wren. Oh my god, Wren."

"No," she yells, kicking at him and trying to get away. "No more, you fucking asshole."

"Wren. Sweetheart, it's me. You're okay. You're safe now." He leans over her, grimacing when she knees him in the stomach. But he's able to push her hair out of her face, holding her head gently. "Look at me, Wren."

It takes her eyes a second to focus, but once she's staring at Rhett and actually comprehending who she's looking at, she bursts into tears. "You found us," she sobs.

"I told you we would," he murmurs, pulling her up and into his lap. "Shit, your hands."

He pulls his knife out of his pocket before reaching around her, cutting through the zip tie. Once her hands are free, she throws her arms around him.

"Rhett," she whispers.

"You're gonna be okay," he says, rocking her back and forth. He holds her tightly, rubbing her back. "We've got you."

Wren's sobs turn into more coughs. Rhett holds her while she tries to catch her breath. His coat is absolutely drenched, but I don't think he cares.

"Sick bastard," Elliot says. When I turn to look at him, I see that he has a bloody-faced, unconscious Jordan tied up and on the ground. He glares at him for one more second before turning in my direction.

The second Elliot's gaze lands on me, it feels like the whole world stops. Bursting into the room the way they did, I'm sure it was a hell of a sight—me tied up and shouting, and Wren half-drowned and unmoving. It was Elliot's worst nightmare come true.

He works his jaw before turning to Rhett. "We're not killing anyone else."

Rhett's nostrils flare. No doubt, he's ready to raze the place to the fucking ground. "Why the hell not?"

Elliot looks at me again, tenderness and worry flashing in his eyes before an undying fury replaces them. "Because first, we're going to make sure they suffer for what they've done."

It only takes a few seconds for Elliot to cut through my zip ties, and then he's pulling me to my feet and examining my body, looking for injuries.

"I'm fine, Ell."

"This doesn't look *fine*," Elliot grits out, pointing to the bruise on my torso. "Or this," he continues, brushing his thumb over a cut on my cheek. "Christ, O." Elliot runs a hand over my hair before pressing a shaky kiss to my forehead. "Fuck."

I squeeze his hands. "We're okay now."

Elliot looks like he has a lot to say, but he keeps his mouth shut. The two of us move to Wren, joining her and Rhett on the floor. Gently, I place a hand on her back, and Elliot brushes his fingers down her arm.

Twisting in Rhett's lap, she looks between the two of us. And somehow, she manages a smile. It may be tearful and shaky, but it's still there.

When Wren reaches for me, I take her into my arms, kissing her cheek softly. Feeling her ribcage expand as she takes a breath calms my nerves. But then we all hear footsteps overhead, and she jumps, clinging to me.

"Fuck." Rhett stands. "We dealt with everyone outside before we came in, but we heard you shouting before we could clear the house."

"I counted three plus Jordan inside before we came down here," I say. "Could be more, though."

Elliot hands me Jordan's gun. "You stay with Wren. Rhett and I will find everyone else."

I nod. The last thing I want is for the four of us to be separated again, but Jordan's men could easily sneak down here and ambush us. None of us are safe until all of his men are eliminated.

So I move Wren from my lap to the floor next to me. We sit side by side, leaning against the trough, our fingers intertwined. Rhett and I exchange a quick glance, and I nod, silently telling him I'm okay. He clenches his jaw, and for a second all the rage he's feeling becomes visible. But then he tamps it down again.

"We'll be back in a couple minutes," he says tightly, and then he turns and helps Elliot carry Jordan upstairs.

Wren leans her head against my shoulder. She's shaking, but at least her breathing has evened out some. If I could, I'd wrap her up in my arms, but I need to be ready to jump to my feet at a moment's notice.

At some point, Wren starts crying again. She tries to stay quiet, so it's mostly sniffles and silent sobs that rack her body. I squeeze her hand, keeping my eyes on the door.

"We're gonna get out of here soon, princess. I promise."

There's movement upstairs, and it sounds like bodies are being dragged across the floor. A few minutes later, footsteps are pounding on the stairs, and Rhett steps back into view.

"It's safe."

Gently, I help Wren up. Her cheeks are covered in tear tracks, her hair is still dripping, and my T-shirt is soaked. Her skin is covered in goosebumps, and she's shivering even worse now.

"We need to get her warm," I say to Rhett.

Rhett tears off his coat. "My shirt is still dry." He pulls his long-sleeved T-shirt over his head, revealing an undershirt underneath. "Sweetheart, take that off. It's practically dripping."

She doesn't move. When I reach for the hem, she recoils.

"Wren?" I say. "What's wrong?"

Stumbling away from us, she shakes her head. "No."

I step toward her. "Princess—"

"Don't." Rhett grabs me by the shoulder and hauls me back. Then he holds his shirt out to Wren, careful not to crowd her. "I understand, sweetheart. It's okay. We'll wait outside the room, and you can get changed down here."

She takes the shirt silently.

Rhett pulls me through the doorway and out of sight. It takes me a second to understand what's going on—that Wren is having a similar reaction to how Rhett acts when he's upset. Being touched is the last thing he wants, and any semblance of vulnerability makes his skin crawl.

And of course Wren is feeling a similar way. It's stupid that I didn't realize it immediately. Someone just took away her ability to breathe, for fuck's sake. Of course she needs privacy.

When Wren steps out of the cellar, she doesn't look at either of us. Rhett's shirt hangs loosely on her, and she's pushed up the sleeves so she can hold her clothes without getting them wet.

I want to hold her. I want to kiss her on the forehead and remind her that she's not alone. I want to pull her into my arms and tell her that everything's okay now, that she's safe, that we'll never let this happen again. But I don't think it's what she needs right now.

We follow her upstairs. In the living room, three men plus Jordan are tied up to what looks like dining room chairs. All of the men are unconscious, and Jordan is just beginning to wake up, a groggy panic setting in.

When Elliot sees us, he tosses me a hoodie. "I had it as an extra layer. You need it more than I do."

I pull it on, thankful for the warmth and the scent of sandalwood and oranges that's always reminded me of afternoons curled up next to Ell while he reads a book.

"Wren," Elliot says.

She tears her gaze away from the men lined up in the chairs. When she looks at Elliot, her expression softens. The fear that was in her eyes earlier disappears, and the clothes she's holding drop from her hands. And then she runs to him, jumping into his arms and burying her face in his neck.

Keeping her in a tight embrace, he says, "I'm sorry it took us so long to get to you, love. Fuck. I'm so sorry, Wren."

She doesn't say anything, just locks her arms around him and lets out a sound that's somewhere between a sob and a whimper. Elliot holds her for a minute while Rhett and I grab some blankets from an over-sized basket in the corner. Then he carries her to the couch, gently setting her down.

"Can we . . ." I hold up the blanket, not sure if she wants to be touched more.

"Yes," she whispers, reaching out to me. "Yes. I just didn't want to be looked at."

"I understand, princess." I unfold the blanket, wrapping it around her shoulders and placing a tender kiss to her forehead.

Rhett places another blanket over her lap, and then he uses another one in an attempt to dry her hair. She smiles up at him when he finishes, but he doesn't return it. He just stares at her, trying to keep himself under control. The man looks ready to set the whole damn house on fire.

"F . . . fuck you."

It comes from Jordan. His head is tilted heavily to one side, like he's too out of it to keep it upright. Blood trickles from his nose, which is definitely broken.

"Goddammit," Rhett says under his breath. He brushes his thumb over Wren's cheek. Then he turns on his heel and stalks over to Jordan. Neither Elliot nor I move to stop him as he kicks Jordan in the face, the force causing his chair to fall back.

Jordan cries out as his head hits the floor. Rhett wastes no time in yanking the chair up. Then he punches him.

"You deserve this," Rhett says, his voice dripping with a venom I've only ever heard when he's talking about Ludo. "How *dare* you hurt her."

"You killed my brother," Jordan rasps.

"You think I give a flying fuck?" Rhett shouts. "You think that justifies hurting an innocent woman? Fuck *you*, Jordan." Another punch. And another. Just as he's winding up for a third, I remember what Wren told me earlier.

"Rhett. Don't kill him."

The glare he gives me sends a chill straight to my bones. And when he delivers his next blow, I realize he has absolutely no intentions of listening to me. I grab him, and he tries to shove me off, but it's a half-hearted attempt. Rhett's angry, but he doesn't want to hurt me. When I pull him away, Jordan is crying and barely conscious.

Elliot stands from where he was crouched next to Wren. "We're nowhere near done with you, you miserable fuck."

Goddammit. I can't hold both of them off.

"Elliot," Wren says, watching him.

"Don't try to stop me, love. No one—and I mean *no one* hurts my family and gets away with it."

"I wasn't going to stop you."

He pauses, reaching out and stroking her face. "What do you need?"

"I want to be the one who kills him," she whispers, looking up at Elliot with a wide-eyed, sincere expression. There's no doubt on her face. No fear. She fucking means it. She *needs* it. "I want him to feel what I did. Every single thing."

Something akin to pride blooms in Elliot's eyes as he smiles down at her. "Of course. Whatever you need."

"And I don't want to watch while . . . while you torture the others. But I don't want to be alone."

Holding his hand out to her, Elliot says, "You don't have to be. Ol, Rhett, can you two handle them?" He gestures to Jordan and his men.

"Absolutely," Rhett replies. "We'll leave Jordan for you, sweetheart."

"I want to take him back with us."

"Then we'll do that."

I brush my lips across Wren's hairline. The fact that she's telling us exactly what she wants without hesitation has a warm feeling spreading through my body. We'd do anything for her, and it's important she knows it.

Still clutching her blankets, she moves to Rhett. His fists are clenched at his sides, his knuckles covered in blood, but he visibly relaxes when her lips meet his in a sweet, chaste kiss.

"I knew you'd come for me," she whispers against his mouth. "I didn't know how soon, but I never doubted it."

He doesn't touch her—probably doesn't want to get blood on the blankets—but he kisses her again. Then he says, "Go. This is going to take some time, but I want to get you home as soon as possible."

Rhett watches her go with a hardened stare. He's barely looked at me since they saved us downstairs.

When I set my plan in motion, I knew I'd be hurting him and Ell. Not only did they have to worry about Wren, but they were scared for my safety, too. I told myself I'd never put them in that type of situation again, but everything changed when Wren came into our lives.

Rhett's angry. And I know Elliot is, too. He's just better at hiding it. But I won't apologize for leading them to Wren sooner. I can't. Because if I'm being honest, I'd do it again.

She looks back as Elliot leads her away, and when she meets my gaze, I smile for her. The light that's usually in her eyes is gone, but it'll show up eventually. We'll help her bring it back.

But first, we need to deal with the men who took it from her in the first place.

Chapter Fifteen

Rhett

Elliot takes Wren upstairs, making sure to keep her wrapped up in blankets. She still looks miserably cold. If I knew Jordan would survive, I'd beat him until he was covered in blood and pissing himself for what he's done to her. But if Wren wants to be the one to kill him, I won't take that away from her—no matter how much I want to.

Oliver has already grabbed a knife from the kitchen. He's tapping it against his palm, eyeing the men in front of us. Everyone is awake now, and all four men look terrified.

Good.

"I'll take him." Oliver nods to the man to the left of Jordan. "You can have the other two."

I was going to claim two of them anyway, so I grunt in agreement.

All of them have their wrists tied to the arms of the chairs. Oliver slams his knife into his guy's hand, smiling when he screams. If I wasn't so pissed off at Oliver, I might smile too.

I look at the two men to the right of Jordan. One has already wet himself, and the other is crying. I'd say it's pathetic, but considering the hell I'm about to put them through, their fear is warranted.

When I step up to the one who's crying, he starts sobbing harder. Slowly, I slice through the front of his shirt, cutting the fabric but not touching his skin. Not yet.

"Those are some nice tattoos you have," I say, staring at the ink stretching across his chest. "Great linework. Wonder what it'd look like if it was done in red."

"Wh-what?" he chokes out, squirming in his seat.

"Your tattoos," I reply, resting the tip of my blade against his skin. "Red. Instead of black."

He shakes his head frantically, and then he whimpers when I drag my knife along a line on one of his tattoos. Blood flows from the cut, staining his skin.

"We were just following orders," he cries.

"Complacency isn't the great excuse you think it is."

"You know how it is, man. I've got bills to pay."

I shake my head. "Not anymore, you don't."

. . .

By the time Oliver and I are done, the floor is soaked with blood, and Jordan has passed out from a combination of injuries and fear.

It's over. Wren's safe. Oliver's safe. But whenever I start to think that his plan worked, that it got us to Wren faster, I remember the way Elliot looked when he realized Oliver was gone. It broke my heart, seeing him like that again.

Oliver tosses his knife to the floor, staring at the mess we've made. I come up to him, grabbing his shoulder and turning him to me. It's the first time I've touched him since I pulled him away from Wren earlier.

"I'm glad you're safe," I say. "But I'm so goddamned angry with you. This was a stupid fucking idea, O. I don't care that it worked. Never *ever* do something like this again."

Oliver remains silent, and a hollow sensation I haven't felt in years expands in my chest.

"Promise me," I bark out.

When he looks at me, the determination burning in his eyes causes me to take a step backward. He follows me, crossing his arms over his chest. Oliver may be shorter than I am, but right now, it feels like he's ten feet tall.

"I'll do whatever I have to," he says. "Whatever is needed to make sure the three of you stay alive. You'd do the same."

"No. This was downright idiotic."

"It was a calculated risk," he snaps. "And I'm sorry for going behind your back the way I did. Truly, I am. But I will *never* apologize for getting to Wren sooner. If I hadn't, we still wouldn't know where she was. She could've died by now, Rhett. And you know you would've done the same thing if you'd thought of the idea. Stop lying to yourself."

"I would never do that to Ell," I shout.

It's then that we realize Elliot and Wren are watching us from the bottom of the stairs. Wren is still wrapped up in multiple blankets, and Ell has a protective arm around her shoulders. They both look exhausted, and Wren's eyes carry a sadness in them that I instantly feel guilty for putting there.

"Rhett, he——" she starts to say, but Oliver cuts her off.

"Don't. If he's going to take his anger out on someone, it's going to be me, not you."

"No," Elliot says. "Right now, our first priority is getting Wren home. So Rhett, calm the fuck down. You two can continue this conversation later."

I bite back my sharp remarks. It doesn't matter that we rescued Oliver and Wren. Tension is still high, and Ell is right. Now isn't the time to fight. It's time to get the hell out of here.

Elliot leaves to grab his car, saying that there's no sense in all of us walking that far, especially since Wren doesn't even have shoes. She sits on the couch, turning so she can avoid the scene in the kitchen while Oliver and I wash off as much blood from our hands and arms as we can.

When Elliot gets back, he carries Wren to the car, gently setting her in the backseat where her change of clothes is waiting. He already has the heat on blast, thank fuck. Wren just got warm again. She needs to stay that way.

After throwing a gagged Jordan in the trunk, I join Wren in the back, and Oliver takes the passenger seat. As soon as everyone is settled, Elliot grabs Oliver's hand, steering with the other. They don't let go for the whole drive.

I pull out my phone and start typing away. First I let Finn know that we made it out safely. Then I contact one of our go-to fixers. He has a team of highly skilled people who can make it look like nothing ever happened at that house. They can do it damn fast, too.

By the time we get home, Wren has fallen asleep with her head on my shoulder. She's still cocooned in blankets, but she found a way to work one of her hands out so she could rest it on my arm.

"Sweetheart," I murmur once we're parked. "We're home."

She stirs, snuggling into me with a moan. "Sleep here."

I can't help but laugh, even though it's pathetic at best. "I don't think so, Wren. C'mon."

She groans, but she opens her eyes, blinking against the bright light of the garage. Elliot opens her door and helps her out, peeling the blankets off of her so she doesn't trip.

Oliver and I drag Jordan through the house and dump him in a guest room. I tie him to the bed, and he tries to say something, but it's incomprehensible with the gag.

Once we lock him in the room, I turn to go, but Oliver grabs my arm.

I pull out of his grasp. "I'm too tired for this right now, O."

"Rhett, please." His tone is worn down, maybe even a little desperate, and it sends chills down my spine. *"Please."*

"Don't beg," I grit out. But it's too late. Memories are already flooding into my mind. The tears, the pleading, the humiliation. The icy fire of hate taking hold of my soul, burning brighter with every incident. "You never have to beg."

I can see it in Oliver's eyes as he realizes what he set off in my head. He reaches for me, but at the last second he pulls back, thinking better.

There are thousands of types of torture. But as Oliver stares at me hopelessly while I try to get my memories under control, I'm reminded that the worst kind of torture is the one that's inflicted by the people you love the most. Or the ones who're supposed to love you but can't find it in them to care.

That's not me. I care. I care more than anything.

"Oliver, I lo . . ." I choke on the words before trying again. "I love—"
But that old voice echoes in my head. *Say it back. Now, boy.*

"Don't," Oliver whispers, shaking his head.

I wish you could get into my head so you could see. So you could understand. I don't want to be like this.

There are words for situations like this, but I don't know what they are. So I grab his head, angling it upward and slamming my lips to his. He fists my shirt at my sides, grunting when I push him against the wall. The kiss is the opposite of sweet and gentle. It's pain and anger and hurt bleeding from both of us, not making anything better and probably making everything worse.

Don't do this to him.

"Fuck." I tear myself away from him, my chest heaving and my heart aching. "Time. I just need time. I'm sorry." My voice breaks on the last syllable.

"Rhett—"

But I'm already out of his reach, in every possible sense of the phrase. I run, the sound of my feet pounding on the floor the only thing I can comprehend until I'm closed in my room and leaning against the door.

I don't let myself stand still. If I stop, I'll stay frozen for hours, replaying everything. My childhood. Almost losing Oliver. And then the absolute nightmare that the past day has been.

In the bathroom, I turn on the shower and step in fully clothed. The water is cold at first, but I barely even feel it. Barely feel *anything*.

I place my hands on the shower wall, bowing my head. The water falls on my back as it warms up, soaking my shirt and eventually my pants.

Slowly, the numbness fades, but it only makes me feel worse. Every thought I was trying to avoid rushes in at once. The taunting. The fear. Leaving but still feeling trapped. And then the terror of losing one of the only people I've ever loved—one of the only people who's ever loved me.

My first sob is so violent that I fall to the shower floor. With my head in my hands, I let go fully, the sounds of my distress echoing loudly in the small enclosure.

How could Oliver do that to us?

And why is a part of me grateful he did it?

I can't stop thinking about Ell and how his eyes were glued to his phone the entire time we were without Oliver. It's like that little blue dot that represented him was the only thing keeping Elliot grounded. The only thing keeping him breathing. Elliot—the one who's always strong and composed and ready for anything—*cried* because he was so scared.

Yet Oliver's plan worked. And based on how terrified Wren was when I got to her, there may have been some truth to his point. It's entirely possible that Jordan would've killed Wren out of anger or miscalculation if we hadn't gotten there when we did.

I rub my chest, trying to soothe the ache in my heart. The truth is that we got to Oliver and Wren in time. We all made it out safely. But my body hasn't caught up yet. It hasn't realized the crisis is over.

Eventually, my sobs die down, but I still don't move. I managed to keep it together for as long as I needed to. But between tonight and all of these old memories resurfacing, I couldn't hold it in any longer. Now I'm too exhausted to get up, and I don't have any motivation to, either.

Maybe I'll just sleep in here.

"Rhett?"

I jump at the unexpected noise. "Fuck."

Through the foggy glass, I can just make out Wren's form where she's standing in the doorway to the bathroom.

"I didn't mean to scare you," she says.

"It's fine," I manage, trying to swallow down the lump in my throat.

"Or interrupt you. Are you . . . are you okay?"

I stare at the water as it flows across the tiles before washing down the drain. *Okay.* It's such an arbitrary way to measure a person's well-being. There are times when I'm okay—when I'm distracted, or when I'm with Oliver and Ell, or on the few days I'm able to control my thoughts. But is that okay? Or is that just barely coping? And if so, then what the fuck am I right now?

"Rhett?" She's closer now, her hand on the shower door. "Can I come in?"

I sigh. "You need to sleep, sweetheart."

"It doesn't sound like you should be alone right now."

Rubbing my face, I mutter, "Fine."

She opens the door, and her expression goes from worried to alarmed. "You're still in your clothes."

I don't have a good explanation, so I shrug.

Wren is in one of her T-shirts and a pair of shorts. It looks like she's showered and ready for bed, but that doesn't stop her from closing the distance between us. She doesn't even hesitate to sit next to me under the spray of water.

On instinct, I lean away from her, so she moves a few inches away to give me space.

"Don't," I say tensely.

"Don't what?"

"Move away."

She scooches back to where she was.

I clench my fists. "But I can't . . . don't—" I let out a frustrated noise. "Jesus fuck."

"Don't touch you?"

I nod.

"I won't," she whispers.

Letting anyone other than Elliot and Oliver see me like this is deeply uncomfortable, but at the same time, I'm glad Wren is next to me. She needs to know what she's getting herself into.

"You're worried about Oliver," I say. "That's why you're here?"

"I'm worried about *you*."

I don't know why, but that makes my heart ache even more. I stare at the water swirling down the drain, unable to look her in the eye. "I get why he did it. And there's a part of me that's glad he did because it means you're safe. We were all acting a little desperate to get you back home."

"Elliot said you were ready to go after Jordan's girlfriend."

I nod. "And I'm glad he stopped me. That could've been a disaster for you."

"And you're angry that Oliver didn't give you a chance to stop him?"

"No. No, I'm angry because I was terrified."

A small noise of surprise leaves her throat. "You thought Jordan would kill him?"

"Sort of," I say. And then I sigh. It's time she hears this story. "When we were nineteen, maybe twenty, we were on a job together. It was pretty simple—sneak in and plant cameras in our mark's house for one of our first clients. Everything was going according to plan until it wasn't. We thought the guy was out of the house when we broke in, but we were wrong. He caught Oliver in his office and had a gun pointed to his head. We were unarmed. Didn't think we'd need to be. Last time we made that mistake.

"We were supposed to meet at a certain point in the house after we finished bugging our respective rooms. But Oliver never showed. When Elliot and I realized he was in trouble, we didn't know where he was or what to do. Oliver was trying to save our asses and pretend he was working alone. He was about to die, and all he could think of was us.

"When we realized what was going on, it felt like someone had carved my heart out of my chest and was crushing it in their fist. Like I was breathing, but I wasn't getting in any oxygen. And then all I could think of was Sammy and how I couldn't save her. How it was about to happen all over again. I was so scared of losing Oliver, I genuinely thought I'd die without him."

"How did you save him?" she whispers.

"We didn't." My throat aches, and new tears fall from my eyes. It takes me a second to regain my ability to speak. "The guy was about to pull the trigger, Wren, and we were absolutely helpless. Just stupid kids who hadn't thought things through enough."

She frowns. "Then how . . ."

"Our mark started having a heart attack. It was freak timing, so coincidental it felt like a dream. But it was very, very real. We left him there to die and got the hell out."

"Oh my god," she murmurs. "If he hadn't had that heart attack . . ."

"Then Oliver would be dead right now. Would've died years ago. Possibly me and Ell, too."

She presses her fingers to her lips, probably trying to think of something to say. The realization on her face tells me that she's getting it, even if she doesn't have the full memory of almost losing Oliver.

"I know I shouldn't hold what Oliver did against him," I continue. "What almost happened all those years ago easily could've happened to you. I just wasn't prepared to relive the fear. Running into that basement, seeing the both of you like that, I was . . ." I shake my head. "I never want to see anything like that again."

"I'm so sorry, Rhett."

I snap my head up so I'm looking at her. "No. No, I'm not telling you this to get sympathy out of you. You needed to know. Almost losing Oliver changed us."

"I know," she says softly.

I run a hand over my soaked hair. "I'll fix things with him. There's no way I couldn't. I just need to . . . process, I guess."

"I understand that." There's a weight to her words that you could only miss if you wanted to. And of course there is. She's been through hell.

I watch her carefully. "How are you feeling?"

"I'll be fine. I came in here to make sure *you're* okay." She yawns, covering her mouth with both hands.

"Hmm. You should be sleeping by now."

"Yeah, about that . . ." Sheepishly, she tugs at her now-soaked shirt. "Could you . . . sleep with all of us?"

"All of us?"

She nods. "Me and Ell and Oliver. And you."

With a frown, I say, "All four of us in one bed? I don't think that makes much sense."

"I know it'll be a little awkward. But I feel safest when I'm with all three of you." Wren has been avoiding my gaze, but now she finally meets it. "And I know you and Oliver are fighting, but he needs you. And you need him, too."

The thought of cramming all four of us onto a mattress doesn't sound like a good way to spend the night, but how can I deny her? And, dammit, I don't want Oliver to feel abandoned either. I'm hurt, but I don't want to put him through any more pain.

"Okay," I say. "We can try it."

I get up and offer a hand to Wren. After hesitating for a moment, she takes it. We stand under the water together, and I push her hair back from her face. When she looks at me, she tentatively places her hands on my chest.

"Is this okay?" she whispers.

"Yes," I murmur. "More than okay."

Gently, I press my lips to hers. She melts into me, her fingers curling into my shirt. There's something about kissing her that makes everything feel a little better. Her lips moving against mine are like a soothing balm to the burning hatred that has a chokehold on my soul. It fades, becoming more bearable in the moment.

No wonder we can't get enough of her.

When we pull away, Wren's eyes are still closed, and a soft smile graces her lips. She looks like she's about to collapse from exhaustion, and hell, that's how I feel, too. So I shut off the water, still keeping an arm around her waist for support.

"Shit," I say, looking down at us. "We're both soaked."

She groans. "How many shirts am I going to go through today?"

Peeling my own over my head, I say, "Hopefully only one more."

By the time I've stripped down to nothing, Wren is still gripping the hem of her shirt, frozen. The same haunted look that was on her face in the basement is back.

Fuck.

"Sweetheart, it's okay. You don't have to take your clothes off with me in here."

She squeezes her eyes shut. "I'm sorry."

"Don't be." I wring my clothes out before tossing them over the glass wall of the shower so they can air dry. "I'll grab you a shirt and leave it on the counter."

"Thank you. I know it's stupid—"

"It's not," I say firmly. "You're allowed all the privacy and space you need."

I towel off quickly before moving into the bedroom and finding her something to wear. She may have already gone through four shirts today, but I don't care. This way she gets to wear one of mine. I like it when that happens—whether it's her, Oliver, or Elliot.

Placing the shirt on the bathroom counter, I say, "I'm going to close the door. Come out when you're ready."

She only takes a minute or two, and then she leads me to Elliot's room with her hand in mine. The lights in the hallway are off, but it's still illuminated. After Wren's first weekend here, we bought a bunch of night lights and put them in the halls. That way she can move through the house without getting scared until she gets more used to the light switches.

Elliot is already in bed with Oliver curled up in his arms. The sight melts away some of the anger that's been consuming me for the past few hours. The whole time, I've been focusing on the pain Oliver caused me and Ell. But I can't deny any longer that he was probably scared, too. He had no guarantee he'd make it out alive, but he did it anyway. For Wren. And I know without a shadow of a doubt that he'd do it for me and Ell, too.

We end up in bed with Oliver and Wren in the middle. She kisses him, and then she leans over him to kiss Elliot. When she settles under the covers, she turns to face me, cupping my cheeks in her palms.

"Thank you," she whispers. "For everything."

I fit my mouth to hers in a silent response. I'm too tired to figure out what to say, especially since I don't want to accidentally make her start crying again. I'm already drawing things out with Oliver. I don't want to ruin things between me and Wren, too.

She drifts off within minutes, and so does Oliver. Elliot raises his head to look at me, somehow reaching over Oliver and Wren to brush his hand down my hip.

"Sleep well, Rhett."

I don't think I will, but I nod. "You, too."

CHAPTER SIXTEEN

Elliot

The mattress moves violently, waking me from the light sleep I just found.

What the hell?

When I open my eyes slightly, I'm just able to make out Wren. She's scrambling into a sitting position, looking at me and Oliver. And then she turns to where Rhett was earlier.

The commotion wakes Oliver. Groggily, he sits up, rubbing his eyes and trying to make sense of what's going on.

"No," Wren whispers, patting the mattress like she'll somehow find Rhett among the folds of the blankets. "Rhett," she cries. "No, no no no. Rhett!"

"Hey. Hey, it's okay. Princess, you're okay." Oliver wraps his arms around her, gently tugging her into his lap.

Rhett has already stood from the armchair in the corner, and now he's moving to the edge of the bed. "Sweetheart, I'm right here."

She doesn't hear him. "How did you survive? Why didn't he?"

"Wren, we're all here. It was just a nightmare." Oliver strokes her back, keeping his voice calm.

Rhett crawls onto the bed. "Hey. I'm here."

When he comes into her view, she sags in relief. "You're alive," she whispers, reaching out to him. "You're here."

"Have been all night, sweetheart." Rhett snakes his arms around Wren and takes her from Oliver, cradling her body to his.

"But you weren't in bed. Where . . . where did you go?"

"I was in the chair, that's all. We weren't fitting on the bed. You and I are both sprawlers, and Ell is a blanket hog."

"Hey! So are you," I say, inching closer to Wren. "What was your dream, love? What happened?"

She shudders, wrapping her arms tightly around Rhett's waist. "You all died. You all died trying to protect me, and then Jordan took me into the cellar, and he forced me underwater for so long that I couldn't hold on for any longer. And then I breathed in the water, and it was horrible and it hurt and I couldn't do anything, but I just couldn't take it anymore."

"Fuck," Oliver mutters. He rubs Wren's back, his fingers hitting Rhett's arm where he's holding her, but neither shy away from the touch. "We're not going to let that happen, princess. You're safe."

She whimpers, obviously trying to hold back tears.

"I won't leave again," Rhett reassures her. "I'll stay in bed."

That seems to calm her down. She nestles her head against his chest, taking in a shaky breath. "Thank you."

Watching Wren try to get herself together brings a question to the front of my mind. "Love. Did you have nightmares last night?"

She nods.

With a sigh, I move closer, my arms coming around her and Rhett. When I see Oliver hesitating to join, I pull him in so all three of us are surrounding her.

"I'm so sorry, Wren," I mutter.

"I'm okay now," she whispers.

But it's pretty damn evident she's not. She's traumatized—rightly so. The memories of the past day or so are going to haunt her for the rest of her life.

We never should've left her alone.

I kiss Wren on the forehead. Her eyes are scrunched shut, and she's clutching Rhett tightly. When I glance between him and Oliver, I find my thoughts reflected in their expressions. We can't let something like this happen ever again.

"Lie back down, sweetheart," Rhett says. "You need to sleep."

We all move to give her some space, settling back into bed quietly. I end up spooning Oliver, and Rhett does the same to Wren. Silently, she finds Oliver's hands and interlocks their fingers. He murmurs something in her ear that I don't catch, but whatever it is, it helps her to fully relax.

She's out in a matter of minutes, and eventually I hear Rhett's breathing even out as well. Slowly, Oliver shifts so he's on his back, still holding Wren's hands. I can barely make out his face in the dark.

"Ell," he murmurs.

"Yes?"

After letting out a long breath, he says, "I know it's hard to understand why I did what I did. But I just didn't want her to be there for a second longer than she needed to be."

"Ol, trust me, I get it," I say in a hushed tone. "It got us to her sooner. And we . . . we almost went to the wrong house. If we had, who knows how long it would've taken us to find her."

"Shit," he whispers.

"I guess what I'm saying is thank you. But please don't do it again."

"I won't," he says quietly. "Because we're never letting Wren out of our sight. This can't happen again, Ell."

"Agreed."

We sit in silence for a moment before he says, "I don't regret it. But I *am* sorry. I didn't want to make you relive what happened all those years ago. But I couldn't let her suffer, either."

"I know."

And really, that's all I can ask of him. Oliver has always been the first to throw himself in danger's way for me and Rhett. Of course he'd do the same for Wren—he loves her, too. It may scare the shit out of me, but it makes me proud of him, too.

"I love you, Ell," he whispers.

"I love you too," I whisper back, kissing his shoulder.

And then we drift to sleep silently, hoping for a better day tomorrow.

. . .

In the morning, I wake before everyone else. It's nice to have all four of us together, even if it's a little cramped. When Wren asked if we could all sleep in the same bed, I was skeptical that it would be comfortable, but I wasn't about to deny her what she needed. Backache be damned, we made it work.

Carefully, I untangle myself from Oliver. He moans but doesn't wake, and I smile when I see that Wren is still holding his hands.

Downstairs, I make a pot of coffee and pour myself a mug. Then I head to the room we're keeping Jordan in. He's awake, although his face is so bruised he can barely get one of his eyes open.

When he sees the mug in his hands, he recoils. "I don't want any of that shit."

"Wasn't offering." I lean against the dresser that's directly in his view, sipping from the mug. I don't say anything else, choosing to stare at him silently.

He squirms. "What are you going to do to me?"

Whatever Wren wants.

But I don't say anything out loud.

The longer I stare at Jordan, the more panicked he gets. It's probably cruel of me to pull this shit, but I can't find it in me to care.

"I'm hungry," he says eventually.

"Did you feed Wren?"

I already know the answer.

Jordan presses his lips into a thin line while he contemplates a response. He must know that lying is a terrible idea—I'd never believe his word over Wren's—and the truth is probably too uncomfortable for him to speak out loud.

"You're a real piece of shit, you know that?" I say.

"I was getting justice for my brother," he snarls.

I laugh bitterly. "Right. Justice for a man who didn't see any value in human life. That's the only way he could willingly take over your uncle's businesses. How many people die at Williams factories every year? How many more can't feed their families?"

"You're a fucking hitman! Don't talk to me about the value of life."

I shrug. "Never said I was perfect."

Jordan rolls his eyes. "You can't stand there and tell me you killed my uncle and my brother because of their ethics. You did it because it paid well."

"Was damn good money, I'll tell you that."

Watching Jordan's face light up with fury has me hiding my smile behind my mug. He's wrong, of course. We didn't take the Williams job for money. We did it to earn more of Ludo's trust. Taking out two exploitative assholes at the same time was an added bonus.

"So this is your twisted sense of justice?" Jordan says. "Torturing and killing my men in front of me? And then doing the same to me?"

"No," I say with a petty smile. "It's yours."

Jordan shifts uncomfortably as he thinks my statement through. And then he sags against the headboard when he finds nothing but truth.

He's the one who was going to torture Wren and kill her in front of us.

He's the one who kept her locked up in an empty room without food or anything to keep her warm.

He's the one who nearly drowned her five times.

"Your treatment of Wren proves that you're cut from the same cloth as your family. She had nothing to do with their deaths. *Nothing.* Yet look what you put her through. You deserve whatever she decides to do, Jordan. Every single thing."

"Bullshit!"

I down the rest of my coffee. Then I smile. "I can't wait to watch you die."

"Fuck you," he spits out.

The longer I stay in here, the harder it's getting to resist the need to strangle him. Wren deserves to have that satisfaction. So I don't bother replying, leaving him alone again and locking the door.

In the kitchen, I make more coffee and pour it into four mugs. I load them all onto a tray and carry them upstairs.

Opening the door to my bedroom is tricky, but I manage it without spilling any coffee. I set the tray on my dresser just as Wren comes out of the bathroom.

She stops when she sees me. "Ell."

I love that she's calling me that.

146

Without hesitation, she runs to me, circling her arms around my waist and pressing her face into my chest. She inhales deeply before letting out a satisfied noise.

"Morning, love." I kiss the top of her head, smiling into her hair.

Wren's always been so openly affectionate toward us. Not only is it endearing, but it's also a relief. New relationships can be awkward, especially when you're still trying to figure out where you stand with each other. But she's rarely backed down from showing us she cares—or from asking for what she needs.

Never be afraid to take, love. Because we'll always give you more.

"You brought us coffee?" she says once she notices the tray on the dresser.

"Yeah. You can have one of the ones with cream."

She wrinkles her nose. "I wouldn't want one of the others."

Chuckling, I say, "You and Oliver both."

She takes a long sip of her coffee before turning back to the bed. Her expression softens when her gaze lands on Rhett and Oliver. They're both wrapped up in each other, a mess of arms and legs and unresolved pain.

"They found each other almost immediately after I got out of bed," she says, twining her fingers with mine.

"I'm not surprised."

She glances at me, a hesitant concern shining in her eyes. "They'll be okay, right?"

I squeeze her hand. "Yeah. We never let our arguments fester for long. It's too miserable. Rhett just needs a little more time, and then they'll be fine."

Our conversation must be too loud, because Rhett groans. His arms tighten around Oliver before he opens his eyes. When he sees who he's holding, his body goes rigid. But then he sighs, pressing his face into Oliver's neck. Oliver stirs, and after another second, Rhett releases him and crawls out of bed.

When Rhett spots us, I already have his coffee in my hands. He takes it groggily, his fingers lingering against mine. Then he touches Wren's shoulder in what's probably supposed to be a soft caress but ends up being closer to a clumsy pat.

She giggles. "Drink your coffee. You need it."

He mumbles something entirely unintelligible, downing half his mug in one go. Grimacing, he rubs his throat. "Hot."

Wren grabs Oliver's mug and brings it to the bed, lowering herself onto the edge of the mattress. "Good morning, handsome."

He gives her a sleepy grin, although I don't miss the extra second it takes for him to find it. "Hi, princess."

Rhett kisses my temple. "I'll meet you guys downstairs for breakfast." Then he leaves, probably heading to his room to get ready for the day.

Oliver slurps his coffee loudly, making Wren smile. The sight warms my heart. Her smiles and laughs may not be as exorbitant, but that's to be expected. As we're able to put more distance and time in between the events of this weekend, hopefully that'll change.

It's sweet to see Oliver trying to make her laugh. I know yesterday took its toll on him, too. And until he and Rhett resolve their issues, he won't be able to get back to being his normal self. But that shouldn't take more than a day or two.

Downstairs, I whip up a quick breakfast of cheesy omelettes and more coffee. Everyone makes quiet conversation, mostly asking the usual, "How did you sleep?"

Apparently, everyone slept as shittily as I did. And if the stiff way Rhett is walking is any indication, staying in bed for most of the night probably left him sore and aching, too.

"Lesson learned," I say, rubbing my lower back. "It was nice to wake up with all of you, but my body can't take it agai-"

I pause when we hear a yell coming from the part of the house where we're keeping Jordan. Wren's smile fades, and her posture goes from open and relaxed to closed off and tense. She hugs herself, chewing on the inside of her lip.

"You okay, love?"

"I forgot he was here."

I set an omelette in front of her, but she doesn't touch it. At some point, we'll have to deal with Jordan. I think all of us would prefer for that time to be soon. But ultimately, the decision is up to Wren. Whenever she's ready.

She stares at her omelette like it's going to jump up and attack her. Then she slips off the stool. "I just need a minute."

The sheer willpower it takes for all three of us not to stop her is astronomical. But we let her go. If she needs a moment to herself, that's understandable. She hasn't gotten one since we brought her home.

My guess is she's heading back to my room. It's in the opposite direction of where Jordan is, and with the distance, she probably won't be able to hear him yelling.

"We need to change things," Rhett says gruffly. He takes a swig of coffee before setting it on the counter harder than he needs to.

"Meaning?" I ask.

"We're not leaving her again. And I don't like the idea of two of us going on long distance jobs while one of us stays with her, either. We work best as a team."

Oliver nods in agreement. "I think she should have a say in what jobs we take. You said it yourself last night, Ell. She's part of our family. And being a part of us means being part of the decision-making process."

"I think we should take it a step further," I say, watching both of them. "Wren can't protect herself. We can teach her to, but it'll take time. So even if we stick with local jobs, I think she should be able to tell us not to take one if it makes her feel unsafe. No questions asked, we drop it. Just like that." I snap my fingers.

Normally, if one of us has a problem with a job that gets sent our way, we talk it through before making a decision. This is similar to that, but it gives Wren slightly more power. And considering she's the one who doesn't have the ability to keep herself safe, I think it's fair.

"I have no problems with that," Rhett says.

Oliver nods. "Same. Whatever she needs."

We eat breakfast in silence. When Wren hasn't come down by the time we've finished the dishes, I set out to find her.

Upstairs, my bedroom door is open. The curtains are still drawn, blocking out the sunlight, but the bedside lamp is on. Wren is sitting on top of the crumpled sheets, leaning back on her hands. The glow of the lamp caresses her skin, wrapping her in warmth.

Since she didn't hear me step into the room, I let myself watch her for a moment. Her eyes are closed, her breathing slow and even. I feel like I'm intruding on a private moment. One filled with the safety of being alone, of knowing no one's watching you. One in which you don't have to perform for anyone.

I knock lightly on the doorframe. "Hey."

She looks at me. The hollowness in her eyes is like a punch in the gut. "Hey."

"You okay?"

"Yeah," she says softly.

I wish you wouldn't lie to me.

Easing onto the bed next to her, I take her hands in mine. "Wren, the past couple weeks have been a lot. It's—"

"I'm fine."

I shake my head. "You're not."

She looks away.

"Talk to me, love."

I run my thumbs across the backs of her hands as we sit in silence. I'm not sure if she's trying to figure out what to say or if she's refusing to talk. It doesn't matter. I'd sit with her in silence for years if that's what she wanted from me.

"What if you were right?" she whispers eventually.

"About what?" I ask, but I already know, and it causes my mouth to instantly go dry. The mournful look Wren gives me has my heart twisting painfully, and I release her hands.

"The three of you have changed my life for the better in so many ways," she says. "It's barely been two weeks, but it's true. I've come to care for you more than I . . ." She trails off, shaking her head. "A lot. I care for you a lot. But what if it's too dangerous?"

"Please don't," is all I can manage to get out. It's like my throat is closing in on itself, like my body is attacking the very notion of what she's saying and leaving me spiraling out of control.

"I can't go through that again, Ell. I didn't think I'd make it that last time. Everything was starting to slow down, and it felt like I was two seconds from losing consciousness. From . . ." She stops, swallowing hard. "You said before that you've made a lot of enemies. Which ones will do worse? Which ones will kill me on the spot?"

"No. No, this won't happen again, Wren."

"You can't guarantee that, and you know it."

"We can."

"You can't!"

"Love." Gently, I take her face in my hands, tilting it so she has to look at me. "The three of us have already discussed it. We're not taking any more jobs that take us away from you for the foreseeable future. Not until you're able to protect yourself. And not until we've killed Ludo and neutralized anyone who's a threat to you. To any of us."

She blinks slowly, frowning. "You'd do that?"

"Of course."

"But . . . you don't have to work?"

"We mostly take jobs for networking purposes and to get closer to Ludo. So no. Money is the least of our concerns. From now on, we won't take any jobs without your personal stamp of approval. We'll run everything by you. And if you're not comfortable with something, all you have to do is say so."

Her hands cover mine as she processes. "You . . . you mean it?"

"Absolutely," I whisper. "We just talked about it, and we're all on the same page."

She inhales deeply, letting her eyes slide closed again. "Thank you."

I kiss her softly in response. Wren sighs into my mouth as I pull her into my lap. Her legs end up wrapped around my waist, her hands running up and down my arms. When we pull away, she rests her forehead against mine.

"I almost got away," she says quietly.

I rub her back, hoping to bring her some sense of reassurance or comfort. "Oliver told me. How did you manage?"

She brushes the tip of her nose against mine. "I tried to think like you do. Oliver says you're always thinking ten moves ahead. So I tried to do that. And I almost made it. I was literally in a car, and I was halfway down the driveway. I just didn't anticipate Jordan and his men coming back with Oliver at that exact moment.

"Maybe it was for the best. If they came back and I was already gone, who knows what they would've done to Oliver. But I was so angry and scared. Jordan was going to kill me. I think he took me escaping as a personal insult to his intelligence. And I understand he's upset because his brother is dead, but that's not my fault."

"I know," I murmur.

"Is it horrible of me?" she whispers. "To want to put him through what he did to me? Does it make me like him? Because I don't want that."

"I don't think so, love. But my moral compass is a little broken."

She lets out a small laugh. "That's fine with me."

"Oh? Why's that?"

Finally, she opens her eyes, pulling away so she can take in my whole face. "Because it means you'll stop at nothing to protect me. I've never had someone like that in my life. Not even my mom. It makes me feel safe. Cared for."

"I'm glad you know it," I say.

As I hold Wren in my arms, my mind starts going over the past two weeks. There's a lot we still don't know about her, but there's one commonality in every situation we've faced with her. For some reason, there's an undying resilience that lies just beneath her consciousness. Based on past conversations, I'm pretty sure she doesn't even see it, but it's there.

It's everywhere—in how she's dealt with her family and Adam, in how she handled the Williams job last week, and in how she refused to give up this weekend even when everything looked hopeless. Her strength doesn't mean she's not hurting, I know that. But I'm damn proud of her.

Wren's stomach growls. She didn't eat a lot last night because she felt sick, so I'd imagine she could eat an entire pantry's-worth of food right now.

"Let's get you some breakfast," I say. "I don't want you to go any longer without food. I also may have left Oliver and Rhett alone together, and we should probably make sure they haven't killed each other."

She nods. And then we head downstairs together, her hand clasped in mine.

CHAPTER SEVENTEEN

Oliver

After Elliot leaves to find Wren, I get up from my stool. "I'm gonna go check on Jordan. Make sure he's not dying or something."

"Not alone, you're not," Rhett says gruffly, moving to follow me.

We walk in miserable silence. It's not often that I wish the floor would open up and swallow me whole, but right now is one of those times.

The way Rhett kissed me last night was so raw and pained that I'm still feeling the aftereffects over twelve hours later. And this morning, I woke up to him holding me—and then immediately leaving me. It was like a stab to the heart, realizing that he held me close while he slept and then pushed me away the second he woke up.

I understand he needs time. No one can turn their emotions on and off like a tap. They ebb and flow, intensify and fade. At this point, it's a waiting game. I just wish it didn't hurt so badly.

In Jordan's room, we find him struggling against the ropes we used to tie him up. His face is bruised and swollen, and his clothes are stained with blood. It satisfies a dark part of me, seeing him like this. It looks like he's in a lot of pain.

"Why are you making so much goddamn noise?" Rhett snaps.

"I have to pee."

Rolling my eyes, I move to untie him, but Rhett grabs my shoulder.

"Don't try anything," he growls at Jordan.

Jordan stops struggling, eyeing Rhett cautiously. Then he mutters, "This is inhumane."

I've known Rhett for fourteen years—four as one of his best friends, and ten as one of his partners. It takes a lot for me to find him intimidating or scary, mostly because I know he'd never willingly hurt me. But the laugh that leaves him is so hard, so callous, that it has me straightening my spine on instinct.

"Inhumane? *Inhumane? Are* you fucking serious?" Rhett yells.

Jordan cowers. "I'm sorry."

"There you go," I mutter. "Apologizing is the first smart thing you've done all weekend."

That seems to make his temper flare. He kicks at the bed, pulling against the ropes. "You three think you're so much better than I am. Look in the fucking mirror. How could you do this—"

The rest of Jordan's sentence is cut off by Rhett slapping him across the face. It's not that hard, but it doesn't have to be. Jordan's face is already such a mess that barely touching it is probably hellish.

We untie him, and Rhett shoves him toward the bathroom, not letting Jordan close the door. There's a window, and there's no chance we're letting him escape.

Once Jordan has finished his business, he reluctantly steps out of the bathroom. Thankfully he doesn't put up much of a fight as we re-secure him to the bed. He just sits there, seeming to have accepted his fate.

As we leave the room, I look back to find Jordan crying silently, his tears falling onto the bed. But I can't find an ounce of pity for him. What he did to Wren is unforgivable.

In the kitchen, I go back to sitting at the counter while Rhett paces. I want to talk to him—no, I want *him* to talk to *me*—but I can't force that. So I pretend to stare at the counter while secretly watching him in my peripheral vision.

"O," Rhett says after a few minutes, stopping in the middle of the kitchen and turning to face me.

"Hmm?" I look up, clenching my fists in my lap where he can't see. *Please tell me you understand.*

"I shouldn't've kissed you."

The food in my stomach sours, and for a second I'm afraid I might actually throw up. I don't know what to say, so I just nod, moving my gaze back to the counter.

It was painful to be close to him like that when he was upset with me, but at least he touched me. At least he was trying. Knowing that he wished it never happened hurts more than the kiss itself did.

"No—Oliver, I'm trying to apologize." Rhett moves around the counter until he's standing close enough to touch me. "It hurt you. I shouldn't've done that. That's what I'm trying to say."

"Okay," I mumble.

"And I'm sorry for running off. And I'm . . ." He sighs. "I shouldn't've gotten so mad, O. I was scared and went straight to being angry instead of trying to understand. You were trying to make sure Wren made it out alive. I can't fault you for that."

The wave of emotions that crashes over me feels like it would've knocked me over if I wasn't already sitting. Ever since I realized how upset Rhett was, it's felt like someone has been slowly wringing my heart out like a sponge. Now all the tension in my body and mind is trying to leave at once.

I rest my head in my hands as tears fill my eyes. Yesterday, I apologized for what I could, but I stood my ground when I needed to. I was so worried that Rhett would never come around.

"I was afraid of losing you," he murmurs, tentatively placing a hand on my shoulder. "It scared the shit out of me. But that's not really an excuse. I'm sorry, O."

As tears fall onto my cheeks, I raise my head to look up at him. He wipes away my tears, his expression turning worried when more replace them.

"You understand?" I croak.

He nods. "I'm sorry it took me so long to see things from your perspective. And I'm really fucking glad that you got us to Wren faster. And that you're both safe."

I grab his shirt, pulling him closer. He holds me and I cling to him as I'm surrounded by the scent of cedar and sage. It's a calming smell, one that's brought me so much comfort over the years. It does the same thing now, even as I soak Rhett's shirt with my tears.

"I love you," I say, holding him tighter when he flinches. "Please don't say it back. Not like this. But I wanted you to know."

"I've never doubted it. Not even once, Oliver."

The urge to be as close to him as possible takes hold of me so strongly that I find myself stumbling to my feet without a second thought. I press my body into his, whispering, "Can I kiss you?"

Rhett nods, running a hand over my hair. There isn't even a split second of hesitation on my part as I fit my mouth to his. This time he's gentle with me, slowly moving his lips against mine in an almost reverent, worshipful way. More tears spill from my eyes, and it makes for a pretty wet kiss, but neither of us care.

"Oh, thank fuck," Elliot says.

I break off the kiss, wiping at my soaked cheeks. Elliot and Wren are standing hand-in-hand at the edge of the kitchen. Wren smiles at me with an odd mix of relief and concern on her features.

"We're okay, princess."

Rhett is still holding onto me, and it couldn't make me happier. I kiss his chest through his shirt before leaning against him. If I could get away with it, I'd never let go.

Elliot makes Wren an omelette, and she takes a couple small bites. Just as Elliot is about to take the frying pan to the sink, she stops him.

"Can you make another one?" she asks.

"I'll make you as many omelettes as you want, love."

"Not for me."

He pauses, giving her a confused look. Then it dawns on him. "For . . . him?"

She nods.

Elliot doesn't ask any questions or try to convince her otherwise. Rhett and I don't, either. Whatever she wants to do to Jordan, we'll let her. And if she decides she wants to feed him, then that's what's going to happen.

Once Wren finishes her breakfast, she takes the omelette and turns to us. "Where is he?"

"I'll take you, princess."

"He stays tied up," Rhett says firmly.

She nods. "I'll feed it to him."

I lead her to Jordan's room, unsure of what to say. Wren's gripping the plate tightly, like maybe she doesn't actually want to do this.

"Can you stay out here?" she says once we stop in front of the bedroom door.

"I don't think that's a good idea."

"He's tied up, right? I'll call for you if I need you."

"Princess . . ."

"I need to do this alone."

"That's the thing, Wren. You *don't* have to do this. He didn't feed you. You don't owe him anything."

"I need to do it for *myself,* O. Please let me."

I don't like it—in fact, I hate it—but Wren doesn't look like she's going to give in. So with a sigh, I unlock the door.

With a kiss on my cheek and a whispered thank you, she steps inside, gives me one last look, and closes the door.

CHAPTER EIGHTEEN

Wren

The second I close myself in the room, a chill runs down my spine. *Maybe this is a bad idea.*

I almost open the door again to tell Oliver I changed my mind, but Jordan's burning glare freezes me in place. It's like he's holding me in front of that trough again, ready to deprive me of oxygen until my body shuts down.

"Your boyfriends said I wasn't going to get any food," he says bitterly. His voice puts me right back in that cellar.

Get it together, Wren. He can't hurt you like this.

"They left it up to me," I reply, lowering myself onto the bed. I use the fork to cut off a small piece of the omelette and then stab it.

"Why are you feeding me?" he demands. "Is that poisoned?"

"When I kill you, it'll be the same way you intended to kill me." I hold the fork in front of his mouth, ignoring his first question. He doesn't need to know the answer. No one does except me.

I want Jordan to suffer. I want him to feel the same fear I felt, to dissolve into the same hopelessness that I did. But there's a difference between him and me—at least, I'm trying to make sure there is. He's the monster here. Not me.

I'll make sure he knows what it feels like to have his entire body screaming for air. But I have to draw the line somewhere. Starving him feels a touch too inhumane.

Grudgingly, Jordan takes a bite. I feed him silently until he's finished the whole thing. When he's done, he glares at me.

"If you think this makes me feel bad for kidnapping you, it—"

"I don't give a shit what you think," I say, standing. "You're not worth the energy."

I leave before he can think of a response.

Oliver is waiting for me in the hallway. He's pacing and wringing his hands. When he sees me, he lets out a relieved breath before taking me into his arms. "I don't think you should go in there by yourself again."

"I was fine."

"Princess—"

I kiss him. All three of them are worried about me, and maybe they have reason to be. I'm a fucking wreck. But I feel stronger than I ever have knowing they're here for me. *With* me. They're changing everything for my safety, and I'll never forget that.

Oliver breaks off our kiss. *"Please."*

"Okay. You can come in next time." I frown. "If there *is* a next time."

"Do you know when you want to kill him?" Oliver asks.

"I . . . I'm not sure."

After I showered last night, I was so tense that Elliot asked me if I wanted to soak in the bath to relax. At first thought, it sounded like a good idea. But when I imagined myself going anywhere near that much water, it took everything in me not to dissolve into panicked tears.

I just told Elliot that I was too tired. There's so much going on in my head, and it feels like too much to dump everything on the guys. Considering I woke up in the middle of the night freaking out from my dream, I'm glad I didn't say anything. Repeated near-drowning or not, I know how to keep my head above water. It's a stupid fear. Embarrassing, honestly. I can get over it on my own.

Still, it doesn't solve my immediate problem. I want Jordan to feel what I felt. But to do that, I have to get close enough to a tub full of water so I can hold him under. Unless I get over my newfound phobia of water real damn fast, I'm not sure what to do.

Sighing, I say, "Can I have a day or two to think about it?"

"Princess, you can have as much time as you need. We're not going to rush you on this." He eases the plate out of my hands.

I tug on my hair. "There's just so much happening in my head. I don't know how to process or stop thinking about yesterday. And all I can remember about Friday evening was making dinner, and then the next thing I knew I was waking up in that room. There's just this . . . blank spot in my mind. I hate it. And I don't know what to do about Jordan because I—because it's just . . . a lot."

"Do you need to talk things out? Ell likes to journal his feelings, but it's not my thing. He always listens whenever I need him. I can do that for you, princess. If you think it'll help."

"That would actually be really nice. I . . . I don't know where to start, though."

He smiles. "That's okay. I'm gonna put the plate in the kitchen and tell the guys what's going on, and how about you meet me in the living room in a minute?"

"Yeah. Okay."

He kisses me on the forehead before heading back the way we came. In the living room, I settle on the couch, staring at the unlit fireplace. Talking to Jordan left me nervous, and I can't pinpoint why.

Maybe because he tried to kill you. And Andrew.

Wrapping my arms around myself, I wonder what Ludo did with Andrew. I'd ask the guys to try and find out, but I'm not sure how they'd react. Especially Rhett. Considering what he did when Adam hurt me, I'm not sure how he'd handle finding out that Ludo could've saved me hours earlier but chose not to.

The last thing I want is for Rhett to do something that could jeopardize their long-term revenge plans. But not telling them that Ludo showed up feels wrong. Really, *really* wrong.

"Princess?"

I look up. Oliver is standing a few feet in front of me, frowning.

"You look like you're going to be sick."

"I . . . I think I'll be okay." My stomach feels a little off and my head hurts, but what else can be expected? I went almost two days without eating anything.

Oliver sinks onto the couch, placing his arm on top of the cushion behind me. "What's on your mind? Do you want to talk about what happened Friday and yesterday?"

I swallow. "Sort of."

He waits for me to gather my thoughts, letting me take my time.

When I'm ready, I say, "I'm feeling a lot of things. I'm angry at Jordan. So, so angry. He took out all of his pain on me when I was barely involved with Tyler's death. I was so scared I wasn't going to make it, Oliver. And when I stepped into that room to feed Jordan—when I looked into his eyes—it was like I was transported right back into the cellar."

"Fuck," he murmurs, his arm falling across my shoulders so he can pull me closer to him. "I knew it was a bad idea to let you go in there by yourself."

"I want to hurt him. I want to kill him. But I'm struggling to figure out where my limits are. What will I regret doing? What will turn me into a monster? Am I already one for wanting to kill him?"

He sighs when I stop for a breath. "Is that why you fed him?"

Nodding, I shift so I can look him in the eye. "I don't want to end up like him."

"We'd never let that happen, Wren."

I find comfort in the longevity of his promise—they'll *never* let that happen.

I want this to be forever, too.

"You're not a monster, Wren. I don't even think I am. Or Rhett or Ell. You're giving Jordan *exactly* what he was going to do to you. I'd say that's justifiable."

"You're sure?" I whisper.

"He took away your power over yourself," Oliver murmurs. "That's unforgivable."

I let his words sink in, doing my best to believe them. Is this what the guys had to go through when they decided to go after Ludo? Did they have to live through the horror of losing Sammy while also trying to figure out if they were in the wrong?

"And while we're on the subject of people taking away your power," Oliver continues, "I want to talk about last night. When Rhett gave you his shirt, and you froze up. I shouldn't've pushed you. You needed privacy, and I completely invaded your space."

I place a hand on his chest. "Thank you for understanding. And it's okay—or at least, I get why it took a second for you to get what was happening. In the moment, I didn't even fully understand what was going on in my head. But I do now. Sort of, anyway."

He cups my cheek, his thumb stroking gently. "What happened?"

Shivering, I say, "I felt so *human,* Oliver. So small and weak and helpless and . . . crushable. And I still feel that way. I can open up to you emotionally without a problem, but the thought of taking my clothes off in front of you or anyone else makes me freeze up. I can't explain it. I trust the three of you with my whole heart, but I just . . . I can't."

"I understand, Wren. It's okay."

I shake my head. "It's not. I don't like it."

"Princess, Jordan tried to take away every shred of your humanity with what he did to you. He wouldn't let you leave that room, he didn't let you eat, he made sure you were uncomfortable and freezing, and he stole your ability to fucking breathe. Of course you're going to have some type of aversion to vulnerability afterward. *It's okay.*"

"But what if I never get over it?" I whisper.

"Do you think it'll change how we feel about you?"

I look away.

"Wren . . . my god, have you been thinking that this whole time?"

"No. Yes? I don't know. Would . . . would it change? What if I never want to have sex again? Because I don't think I can. Not right now."

"Wouldn't change a thing," he says. Doesn't even hesitate. "*But* I don't think that's going to be a problem. You've just been through hell. Give yourself space. I'm sure as time passes, you'll figure out what you need to get comfortable with that level of intimacy. And until you're ready—until there's absolutely no doubt in your mind that you want it—we have no problem waiting. I think we've made that clear."

"You have," I whisper, running my fingers over the soft fabric of his sweater. "It means the world to me."

"You mean the world to us, princess. And when I say you, I mean *you.* Your mind and your heart, not just your body. I love all of you, and I'm pretty sure I will forever. Whether I have sex with you again or not."

Oliver's reassurances melt my heart, but they do something else, too. For the first time since I woke up in that empty room on Friday night, I feel like I have some control over myself again. Not only is it a relief, but a sense of safety falls over me as well.

I took this conversation to what's probably an unlikely scenario for me—no sex ever again. But Oliver didn't even skip a beat. No negotiations, no pleading, no anger or entitlement. Just flat out acceptance. It's a comforting reminder that with the three of them, I'm the safest I've ever been.

An idea sparks in my mind. A possibility, even if it's one that'll take some thought.

"I might know what I need," I say hesitantly. "I'm not sure. I want to think it over for a few days. But if I'm right, would you be willing to help me?"

Oliver stills, his expression softening. "Of course."

"Thank you."

I kiss him, running my hands over his hair and clasping them at the back of his neck. With a smile against my lips, he snakes an arm under my legs and pulls me onto his lap.

Three times now, Oliver's told me he loves me. We chatted a little on Fridays at the coffee shop, but it's only been two weeks since we've started getting close. Yet this man is *in love* with me. He said he'd die a thousand deaths for me if it meant I got to live.

It all feels so overwhelmingly fast, but at the same time all three of them feel so *right*. I've learned so much about Elliot, Rhett, and Oliver over the past couple weeks. Much more than I would've if we hadn't been thrown into multiple stressful situations.

I'm not sure I'm ready to say the words back, but when I don't, Oliver doesn't look even a little disappointed. It's like he said he loves me with the sole purpose of making sure I know. There's no ulterior motive, no expectation of me saying it back.

How? How did I get so unfathomably, unbelievably lucky?

Elliot peeks into the room. "Hey, sorry to interrupt. I was thinking of swinging by your apartment and grabbing some of your stuff. Can you make me a list of everything you need?"

"Oh. Yeah, sure. Thank you."

"No problem, love." He pulls his phone out of his pocket and hands it to me. "You can make the list on here. I'll make sure to bring your phone back with me. Fuck, we'll need to get you a new one too, O."

I start typing away, trying to think of everything I'll need. I'm not sure how long I'll be staying here, but I definitely don't want to be alone for the foreseeable future.

As I make the list, my mind goes into planning mode, thinking of all the things I need to do.

Ava's probably texted me a thousand times, so I'll need to reply to her.

Am I going into work tomorrow? I feel like that's a bad idea.

It's a new month, so I'll need to—

Shit. It's a new month.

"Oh my god," I say, shooting up straight in Oliver's lap. "I didn't pay my rent yesterday."

"You were a little occupied, princess," Oliver says.

"No, you don't understand. They're really strict about it. I can't be late. I can't—" I stop when I notice Oliver and Elliot exchanging a meaningful glance. "What?"

"We, uh . . ." Oliver chuckles nervously. "We took care of it."

"You . . . what?"

"Your rent is paid for the rest of your lease, love."

My mouth opens and closes on its own accord, like it's trying to say something. But my brain hasn't caught up yet, so all that comes out is, "Huh?"

With an amused smile, Elliot comes to crouch in front of me and Oliver. He takes one of my hands, kissing my knuckles. "We meant to tell you. Actually, we meant to ask you first. But then *someone* got a little too excited and skipped a couple steps of our plan."

"Hey! You make me sound like a little kid," Oliver whines.

I laugh. It's such typical behavior—all of it. Of course they paid my rent. Ever since that Friday two weeks ago, they've done everything they possibly can to take care of me. And Oliver jumping the gun is so him that I'm not even surprised.

"I probably would've said no," I mutter.

"And that—" Oliver says, poking me in the side, "—is *exactly* why I didn't wait to ask you. Every time money comes up, you get this really stressed out look on your face. I don't like it."

"What? No, I don't!"

Elliot squeezes my hand. "You're a horrible liar, love."

"I'm not!"

"You have multiple tells," Oliver says with a snicker. "We figured them out pretty damn fast."

I sputter, trying to think of a reply, but I end up laughing into Oliver's sweater, clutching the fabric with my fist. When I stop, I find both men staring at me. Elliot looks relieved, and Oliver looks like . . . well, he looks like a man who's hopelessly in love.

Gently, I kiss them both. Then I say to Elliot, "Do you want me to come with you? To the apartment?"

"Only if you want, love. It might help you remember what happened Friday night when you got kidnapped."

"Oh, that'd be nice." I start to get up.

Oliver's arms lock around my waist. "That's not a good idea, Wren."

"What? Why not? If I remember—oh." I sag against him. Because while I hate not knowing what happened Friday night, I'm not sure I'm ready to remember. What if something horrible happened? Can I handle that right now? I don't think so.

"Why don't you give yourself some time, princess? Let yourself recover and work through everything you're feeling now before adding something else to the mix."

"I suppose that makes sense," I mutter.

Squeezing me gently, Oliver says, "Is Rhett going with you, Ell?"

"No. He wanted to stay in case you two needed anything."

Oliver frowns. "You're going by yourself."

"I'll be fine, O."

"I'm coming with you." Oliver kisses my temple before lifting me off his lap and setting me on the couch. "You'll be okay, princess?"

"Yeah. Thank you for listening to me."

"Whatever you need," he murmurs. Then he gives me one last kiss before he leaves with Elliot.

For a few minutes, I sit in silence, going over everything I said to Oliver. I feel a little better, but there's still so much weighing on my chest. Why didn't I tell Oliver that Ludo showed up and left me? How am I supposed to get over my fear of water? What if I'm never able to recover from what Jordan put me through?

No. I can't let that happen. I won't let that happen.

Without another thought, I stand from the couch and head upstairs. In Elliot's bathroom, I close the door, leaning against it. Starting with the tub is a disastrous idea. It's too big and intimidating. So I move to the sink, turning on the water.

It flows down the drain, and for a second I stand as still as a statue, making sure I'm ready for this. But the thing is, if I wait until I'm comfortable, I don't think I'll ever move forward. So I close the drain and let the sink fill up.

Once there's an inch or two of water in the bowl, I dip my fingers into it, letting the warmth ground me. So far, so good.

"You can do this," I tell myself, staring at my distorted reflection on the surface. "You have nothing to be afraid of."

But as the level rises, my heartbeat quickens and my thoughts turn against me.

Freezing cold.

He's not going to let me up.

I need air. I can't hold on.

I'm going to die like this.

I shut the tap off before stumbling away from the sink. My back hits the wall, jarring me, and I finally tear my eyes away from the water. I fix my gaze on the floor. Sturdy. Solid. Safe.

My vision is blurred at first, but as my heartbeat slows, the white tiles come into full focus. Raising my head, I stare at my reflection in the mirror. My eyes are wide, and my breaths are short pants.

A realization hits hard, like a blast that threatens to topple me.

I can't kill Jordan.

But almost immediately, a second realization enters my mind. This one steadies me and washes down the panic that's still trying to claw its way up my throat.

But I know someone who can.

. . .

It takes me a while, but I find Rhett in what looks to be the library. He's standing over a desk, glaring at an open laptop like it's done something to personally offend him.

As I cross the room, he looks up. His gaze sweeps over my body, taking in every little detail. Apparently, he's not satisfied with what he finds.

"Did something happen?" he asks, still looking me over with a hardened gaze.

"What?"

"You look worse than you did last night. Did something happen?" He's already halfway across the room, meeting me in the middle and pressing the back of his hand to my forehead. "Are you feeling off? Have you been drinking water?"

"I woke up with a headache," I mutter. "And my stomach feels a little weird, but I figure that's normal. I think I'm okay."

"How much water did you drink while Jordan had you?" He sighs. "Never mind. I know the answer."

He leads me to the desk, grabbing a glass of water that's next to his laptop and handing it to me. I take a few sips. When he gives me a disapproving glare, I drink some more.

"I had some water," I say after I've drained most of the glass. "From the bathroom sink of the room I was locked in. But I didn't think about it a lot."

He nods, still frowning. Again, he looks me up and down. "I'm calling our doctor."

"What? I don't think—"

He holds up his hand to shush me, already tapping buttons on his phone. "We should've done it last night, or at the very least this morning. Fuck. We were all too preoccupied to think straight."

"Rhett, you don't . . ." I trail off with a sigh, watching him bring his phone to his ear.

He has a short conversation, and I can just make out a masculine voice on the other end. When he hangs up, he says, "He'll be here in an hour. Christ, Wren. Sit down. You look like you're going to pass out."

I do, sinking into the chair behind the desk. Rhett stays close to me, checking my temperature with the back of his hand again and frowning.

"I'm okay," I mutter.

"The doctor will decide that. Fuck. We shouldn't've given you coffee this morning. That's not going to help get you hydrated."

I shrug off the thought, mostly because Elliot bringing us coffee in bed was really sweet. With a sigh, Rhett leans against the desk. I scooch the chair forward so our legs are just barely touching.

Nodding to his laptop, I ask, "What were you up to before I came in here?"

He narrows his eyes, crossing his arms over his chest. "You're not getting out of answering my question."

"Wha . . . what?"

"Did something happen?"

I frown. "I'm probably just dehydrated. And tired."

"Don't think I can't tell the difference between a physical ailment and an emotional one, sweetheart. You're obviously suffering from both. So I'd advise you to stop avoiding my question."

Jesus. Maybe I really am a horrible liar.

Drumming my fingers against the desk, I say, "I'm just not sure what to do about Jordan. It's weird having him here."

"Is it scaring you? Having him in the house?"

"Not exactly."

"Then what's going on?"

"I may need your help," I say grudgingly. "Killing him."

"You don't want to do it?"

"I'm . . . nervous."

Obviously, the guys would never let me drown Jordan alone. They'll make sure he won't ever touch me again. And if by some accident I end up falling into the water, they'd pull me out immediately. I don't have any reason to be scared. But it's too much. I just *can't*.

"It's your first kill," Rhett says. "I'd say it gets easier from there, but it depends on the type of person you are. And who you're killing."

"Hmm." That's not my problem, but I don't tell Rhett that. It's too stupid, and he's already worried enough about me.

"Are you asking for my help, Wren?"

Biting the inside of my cheek, I nod. I stare into my lap, too afraid that if I look at him, he'll see exactly why I can't do this on my own.

"Sweetheart." His tone is gentle as he brings himself to his knees in front of me. The position is one he hates, although I'm not sure why, but he does it without a second thought.

"Yes?" I whisper.

"I'll gladly do it. You want me to carve his heart out of his chest and give it to you, I will. You want me to hold his head under water repeatedly until you feel like you have justice, I'll do it with a smile on my face. My will is yours, Wren, and these hands—" Rhett holds them out to me, "—will do whatever you direct them to."

I place my hands in his, and he brings them to his lips, kissing each of my fingers. Maybe I should be deterred by a man who's so willing to kill for me, but instead I find myself smiling down at him.

"Thank you."

"Anything, Wren. Anything."

The force in his voice has me closing the distance between us. Leaning down, I fuse my mouth to his in a grateful kiss. His hands rest on my thighs, and I stroke my fingers over his hair with a moan.

"You mean more to me than I ever thought I could feel toward a person," I whisper when we pull away. I brush my nose against his.

Something fearful crosses Rhett's face, but he schools his expression before it's even been a full second. "I know, sweetheart." Then he stands, looping his arm around me and picking me up.

I grab onto his shoulders with a surprised laugh. "What are you doing?"

"I have some work to do," he says, sitting in the chair and settling me on his lap. "You're not leaving my sight until you've seen our doctor. And in the meantime, you're finishing that glass of water."

"It's okay that I'm on your lap? If you don't want that much touching—"

"I want you close, Wren." He brings one arm around my waist, typing on his laptop with one hand. "Reminds me that you're safe."

"Okay," I whisper.

I dutifully sip my water, trying my hardest not to squirm too much as he works. He seems to be doing a mixture of answering emails and adding a variety of numbers, notes, and links to a colorful spreadsheet. Part of me wants to ask what it is, but the rest of me is absolutely enraptured by the way Rhett looks when he's focused. He's hardly blinking, that's how caught up in his work he is.

When the doctor arrives, he checks me over. It's a lot of poking and prodding that I want to shy away from, but it's a necessary evil, so I grit my teeth and deal with it. Rhett holds my hand the entire time, explaining to the man what happened.

"She went without eating from Friday morning to late last night. Barely had any water, was potentially hypothermic for some of that time, and was also nearly drowned five times."

The doctor looks up at Rhett, alarmed. "Five times? What the hell? Mr. Brooks, that's—"

"I'm not paying you ten thousand dollars for you to do anything but mind your own damn business and keep your mouth shut. You know that. Is she going to be okay?"

I choke on air. Ten thousand dollars?!

How much money have they spent on me?

Oh god, I think I'm going to be sick.

"I'm well aware of my position, but if you're hurting her, then I can't just stand by and let that happen. Are you holding her captive? Or is this a sex thing? Or—"

"It wasn't them," I cut in. "They saved me."

My voice isn't convincing, mostly because I'm still recovering from the shock of how *expensive* this is. The doctor narrows his eyes, watching me briefly, before gathering his things.

"Her lungs sound fine. No persistent cough, miss?"

"No."

"Then you'll be fine in a day or two. Drink lots of water, don't skip meals, and make sure to get plenty of rest. And please—stay away from bodies of water."

Oh, I plan on it.

With a half-hearted smile, I say, "Thank you."

The doctor turns to Rhett. "You want me back in two or three days to check on her?"

"Definitely."

"Will do."

Once he's gone, Rhett starts fussing over me again. It's too sweet to be annoying. Just as we finish eating lunch, Elliot and Oliver come inside, carrying my duffel bag and a backpack I normally keep under my bed. Elliot also has a familiar-looking box tucked into the crook of his arm.

"My book!" I rush over to him, ignoring the way it makes my head all fuzzy, and open the box with a grin.

Elliot lets out a relieved sigh. "I wasn't sure if you'd like it."

"It's one of the best gifts I've ever received, Ell." I stand on my tiptoes and peck him on the cheek. "Thank you."

"It's the least I could do," he says, sweeping me into his arms and capturing my mouth with his.

If this is the least he can do, I can't help but wonder what the most is. But then I realize I already know the answer to that.

Anything.

I nuzzle my face into Elliot's chest before glancing between them. "You three are the best."

Oliver winks at me. "Trust me, princess. We know."

CHAPTER NINETEEN

Wren

I take the week off from work. My boss isn't too happy about it, but I tell her it's a family emergency and I don't have a choice. Hopefully that doesn't come back to bite me in the ass later.

We barely leave the house. The guys make sure I get enough to eat and drink, and Rhett refuses to let me have coffee until the doctor declares me re-hydrated. Oliver lets me have a few sips of his while Rhett isn't looking, though.

None of them push me about sex. Hell, they don't even mention it. Oliver explained how I'm feeling to Elliot and Rhett so I wouldn't have to hash it all out again, and they understand completely.

After a few days, I'm feeling much more like myself. My headache is gone, my stomach is back to normal, and I'm not feeling dizzy anymore.

Emotionally, I'm still unsteady. I'm having nightmares every night, although I never wake up alone. And at least once a day, I have to remind myself that I'm not trapped in that room anymore, waiting to die.

I think it's why I haven't dealt with the whole Jordan situation yet. After I froze up Sunday morning when I went to feed him, I haven't gone into his room. The guys have kept giving him food, which they're not happy about, but they're not pushing back against my wishes.

The guys haven't pressured me to put an end to Jordan's misery. They're letting me take this at my own pace. When Rhett kills Jordan for me, I don't want to feel weak and small. I want to feel strong. Because when Jordan dies, I want him to know that this isn't just the guys' anger. It's mine, too. *I'm* the one who wants him dead. This is me taking my power back, as Oliver put it. I have a feeling I'm going to be doing a lot of that lately.

In fact, it's what I'm about to do right now. I've spent a couple days thinking about what Oliver and I talked about, and my idea has solidified into a full-fledged plan. The first step is to talk to Elliot.

I find him in his office. He's sitting at his desk, staring at a spreadsheet on his computer that looks like the one Rhett had pulled up the other day.

"Ell?"

He looks up. "Hey, love. Need something?"

I nod. "Um. Ropes?"

Frowning, he says, "For Jordan? He's already restrained."

"No, for . . . Oliver." I can feel heat rushing through me as I say it.

With a chuckle, he stands and takes my hand. "He'll like that."

In his room, Elliot pulls out a variety of ropes for me. I take what I'm pretty sure I need, gathering them up in my arms. Before I can go, Elliot stops me.

"I know Oliver wouldn't force you into anything. But are you feeling pressured?" He cups my chin, his thumb brushing over my cheek. "You don't have to have sex if you're not ready to yet."

"Not feeling pressured." I lean into his palm. "But I'm not going to sit around and wait until I *maybe* feel comfortable again. I'm going to figure out what I need and take things at my own pace. And Oliver is going to help me. If I need to stop, I will."

Elliot smiles. "That's my girl."

His praise warms my heart, and I stand on my tiptoes to kiss him. "I'll see you when we're done."

I don't bother trying to look through the whole house to find Oliver. He got back from a makeup lunch with his mom about an hour ago, so he could be anywhere. I shoot him a text, and he tells me he's in the living room. When I step into the room, I see him on the couch facing away from me.

"I know what I need," I say.

Oliver turns, and his gaze sweeps over the ropes in my arms as a slow grin takes over his face. "Every day, I find yet another similarity between you and Ell."

"Is that a compliment?"

"Oh, definitely. I'm in love with the man, after all." He gets up and comes around the couch so he's standing in front of me. "You're sure you're ready?"

I want to feel strong.

"I'm positive."

He gestures to the rope. "Explain your thought process here. I'm curious."

"It's about power," I say. "Power and control."

He nods slowly, narrowing his eyes. "Okay."

"My issue is with vulnerability, right? With feeling too exposed or too human or too unsafe. But if I feel like I'm in charge, I think a lot of that will fade."

"I'm pretty sure I'm following."

"I don't want you to touch me without my permission. And I want you to do what I say. I want to have all the power this time. As long as that's okay with you."

"Wren," he murmurs, "it'd be an honor. And a dream come true, but that's beside the point."

I smile. "Then let's go."

In Oliver's room, I lay out all the ropes on his dresser. Nervousness curls in my belly as I turn to face him.

"Um. I've never done this before. Been . . . in control."

"Never wanted to until now?"

"No, I have, I just . . ." I grimace. The last thing I want to do is bring up Adam and my family, but there are so many things from my past that are still affecting me.

"Just what, princess?" Oliver squeezes my hand reassuringly.

"Adam didn't like that I wanted to be in control. I think I made him feel emasculated or whatever."

"Well, Adam is a stupid fuck."

I giggle. "He is. But I still have him in the back of my mind, you know? I'm afraid of getting shot down, or of doing a bad job and being a failure. I know it's stupid. And I know the three of you would never be judgmental or impatient or make fun of me. But . . ."

"It's the type of thing he would do," Oliver finishes softly.

I nod. "It's not that I don't trust you. I just don't know how to get past the anxiety."

Oliver laughs. "I understand that better than most."

"I know," I murmur.

"Do you know what you need to feel comfortable? Is it reassurance? Because I won't make fun of you. And, just to be clear, I'm not expecting you to dom in the way Ell does—or in the way Rhett does. I want to see how *you* take charge. And I'm here with you every step of the way while you figure that out."

"I don't want to call you names or be mean to you. I'm pretty sure I wouldn't like that."

"You don't have to do anything that'd make you uncomfortable, princess."

"And I don't want to take all my clothes off. I—I have something I'd like to wear."

"Whatever you need," he whispers, taking my hands in his.

Oliver's tone is so gentle and reassuring that I can't help but relax into him. After a quick kiss, I head into the bathroom and get changed. I'm nervous, but I'm also excited.

Before stepping back into the bedroom, I check myself in the mirror, admiring the dark red babydoll nightgown and matching panties I chose. It opens in the front, revealing my stomach and kissing the tops of my thighs. It makes me feel pretty and confident while still covering enough skin that I don't feel overexposed.

Part of me thinks it's silly that I don't want to be completely naked in front of Oliver, but I can't help the way I feel. I trust him—I trust all three of the guys. But I'm just not ready yet.

"Baby steps," I whisper to myself. Then I open the door.

Oliver smiles when he sees me. He's sitting on the edge of the bed, leaning back with his hands on the mattress. "Absolutely beautiful."

I stifle the nervous giggles that threaten to overtake me. When Oliver stands and starts moving toward me, I blurt out, "Wait."

He stops, backing up until his legs hit the bed. "Did you change your mind?"

I swallow hard. Shake my head.

"Okay. You know you can, right? You have all the power, princess."

"I know," I whisper.

He smiles, waiting patiently, and I realize he's undone the top buttons on his shirt. His butterfly tattoo is just peeking through the opening, and it's sexy as hell.

I almost laugh. This man—this hot-as-hell, strong, ruthless man is submitting to me. *Me.*

You have all the power, princess.

Rolling back my shoulders, I clear my throat. Oliver raises an eyebrow in anticipation.

"Crawl to me."

Lust ignites in Oliver's eyes as he lowers himself to his knees. Slowly, he crawls to me, holding my gaze as he makes his way across the carpeted floor. His immediate obedience helps me relax, and the sight of him in this position has my heart beating in an erratic pattern.

He stops at my feet, staring up at me. Waiting for my next command.

"Put your hands behind your back," I whisper.

He does, shifting his weight so he's sitting on his heels.

"Now take my panties off."

Oliver licks his lips before he scooches forward on his knees. His breath is warm against my skin as he places a worshipful kiss to my lower stomach. Then he latches onto my panties with his teeth and gently tugs them down my legs. He keeps them in his mouth after I step out of them, grinning at me.

I giggle. "You don't have to do that."

He lets them fall. "You smell so sweet, princess. My mouth is practically watering."

"You can wait."

He groans.

"You're okay with me tying you up?"

All four of us touch each other a lot, whether it's a quick kiss on the forehead or a brush of fingers across an arm. None of that's bothered me since we got back. But I'm worried that it'll be different during sex. That one of them will touch me somewhere unexpected, and it'll make me feel too vulnerable. I'm hoping that having Oliver's hands tied will help me ease back into things.

"More than okay. How do you want me?"

"Just sit on the bed and hold out your wrists for now."

He obeys. I tie his wrists together, making sure that the ropes are secure but not too tight. Then I crawl onto his lap, straddling him. He doesn't touch me—doesn't even move except to kiss me back when I press my lips to his. I nip at his bottom lip, and he groans. Then I grind lightly against his erection, adding just enough pressure to tease us both.

"Fuck," he mutters when I pull away. Oliver's eyes are half-closed, like he's already high off of us and this moment. When I rub his dick through his pants, his breath hitches.

"I'm going to get these off of you," I say. "And then you're going to lie back, and I'm going to sit on your face until I come."

"Fuck. Yes. Please, Wren. I've been dying to taste you."

"Dying, huh?"

"I'm not joking," he says, and he's so serious that I actually believe him. "Every time I think about having my tongue deep inside you, I need you. Immediately. As much as I need fucking air."

Holy shit.

I slide off his lap. Getting his pants and boxers down his legs is a little hard since he can't lean on his hands, but we manage. Then I point to the bed, and he lies down on his back.

"Good boy."

Oliver whimpers.

I can't help but smile. Having Oliver taking orders from me is different and new. I'm nervous—I don't want to do anything that'll make him uncomfortable. But I also trust him to tell me if I push past one of his boundaries.

On the bed, I lean down and run my tongue across his bottom lip before I pull away. "Ready?"

"Please," he whispers. "Fucking suffocate me."

I move into position and lower myself onto his face. I face his legs so if I decide to sixty-nine we can, but for now I want all of Oliver's focus on me.

He parts me eagerly with his tongue, lapping at my arousal and spreading it to my clit. He circles it gently with a deep moan, like he's eating his favorite meal for the first time in years.

"Oh, just like that," I say, unable to stop myself from grinding against his face.

He groans, continuing to work me over with his tongue, and part of me wishes his hands were on my hips.

Good. That's good.

I don't move to untie him, though. I still don't want to be touched, just in case. The guys have always been in control during sex. I'm afraid my mind will default to that. From there, I'll slip right into the way Jordan and his men grabbed me and shoved me around. Or how I couldn't get my head above water no matter how hard I tried, couldn't get any air—

"Wren. Wren, relax." Oliver has stopped his ministrations. "Princess, take a breath."

I gasp, coming back to reality. "Oh my god."

"Do you need to stop? It's okay if you do."

"No, I just started . . . thinking. But I'm fine."

"You're sure? You want me to keep going?"

I find his hands with my own, interlacing our fingers. It's a little awkward considering his wrists are still tied, but he doesn't complain. "I'm sure."

Oliver starts off slowly, gently tracing his tongue around my entrance before he sucks on my clit. I moan, my fingers tightening around his.

I let myself get lost in the sensations. Any time my mind wanders, I squeeze Oliver's hands, and he squeezes back. It's the gentle tug I need to pull me back to the present.

For the next ten minutes, Oliver doesn't slow down at all. It's like he can't help himself. Considering the desperate sounds of pleasure coming from him, he really does need this. The thought has me careening toward an orgasm so hard my legs begin to tremble.

"Oliver, I'm gonna come," I gasp.

Normally, he'd pull away and edge me until I can't think straight. But not this time. No, he continues working me exactly the same way, his fingers tightening around mine. And then my vision goes blank as pleasure shoots up my spine, exploding through my veins. I have to fight to keep my balance as I reach my peak. And then I come crashing down, panting and shaking.

"You taste like heaven, princess," Oliver mutters, nuzzling his face against me. "God, I never want to stop."

"Careful what you wish for," I say in a teasing tone.

He groans. "I think I've made it pretty clear that whenever you're concerned, *careful* flies right out the window."

Oliver sucks on my clit, causing me to cry out. He probably meant it to be a distraction so I don't think too hard on what he just said, but it doesn't work. It's true—he *was* reckless. All he cared about was getting to me sooner. *Because he loves me.*

I move off of him, turning around and straddling his waist.

"Wren, what—"

I take his face in my hands and kiss him hard. My taste explodes on my tongue, and as Oliver matches my enthusiasm, I can't help but moan.

"I want you inside of me," I whisper.

I scooch downward, taking his dick and stroking it slowly. Oliver thrusts his hips upward with a groan, and I stop.

"Please keep going," he pants. "Shit."

"It's cute when you beg," I say lightly, smirking at him.

He lets out a grudging laugh. "This is what I get for teasing you all the time, huh?"

I start stroking him again. "Mmhmm."

"Worth it," he says with a wink.

I guide his cock to my entrance, taking him in an inch. A whimper escapes my mouth at the way he feels. I mean to take it slow, but I can't help myself as I sink down until he's all the way inside of me.

"Wren," Oliver groans. His hands are clenched into fists on his stomach. When I start moving up and down, he lets out something like a high-pitched shout.

Fuck, that's hot.

I set a steady pace, rubbing my clit gently.

"Christ, Wren," Oliver says. He rolls his hips again, but the look I give him makes him stop. "Fuck. How am I supposed to stay still? Too good, princess."

"Do as you're told, or I'll stop."

He whimpers, clenching his fists even tighter. I wasn't sure how I'd feel about having him like this. Most of me was sure I'd like it, but the rest was clouded over with nervousness and self-doubt. But god, now that he's underneath me and completely at my mercy, I wouldn't trade this for anything.

Not only do I feel safe and in control, but I feel strong for the first time in days. And it's right then, just as I come again, that I realize I can handle everything I've been putting off. Not on my own, but with Elliot, Rhett, and Oliver by my side.

When I come down, Oliver is staring at me so softly, so sweetly, that I find myself leaning down and kissing him without making a conscious decision to do so. It's instinct, maybe, or an irresistible pull to him that I can't explain. Either way, the kiss is overflowing with hundreds of emotions and thousands of unspoken words. It takes my breath away, and when I break the kiss, Oliver looks like he's barely holding on for dear life.

"You," he pants, "are a sex goddess."

I giggle at the notion, moving back to an even pace now that I'm not distracted by our kiss.

Oliver groans, pushing his head into the mattress. "So close, Wren. So close."

"Mmm. You want to come, O?"

He gives me a playful look, repeating something I once said to him. "What do you think?"

The laugh that bubbles up my throat is like a release of its own. "It's like that, huh? You want to come? Then beg for it." I start moving my hips in a different way, trying to keep him on the edge without pushing him over.

"Wren, please," he groans.

I wait for a second, but he doesn't say anything else. "I happen to know the men you've been sleeping with for the past ten years. They would never call that begging. Try again."

He grins. "Was hoping you'd take pity on me."

"I'll take pity on you once you've pleaded hard enough."

Holy shit, this is fun.

Oliver blows out a breath. "I want to come so bad, princess. Please."

I raise an eyebrow.

"Wren, please. I'm begging you, let me come. I want to come inside of you. God, I want it more than anything right now. Please."

"Such a good boy," I murmur, picking up my pace again.

Oliver grunts, and then his eyes widen. "Oh, fuck."

"Give it to me, O. Give it all to me."

He lets out something between a groan and a whine while his whole body tenses. "Wren. Oh my god, Wren."

"Eyes on me while you come, Oliver. I want to see."

Our gazes meet, but his eyes are unfocused with pleasure. I move my hips slower, drawing out the moment until he's finished. When he melts into the mattress, I slowly lift myself off him. Then I pepper tiny kisses up his body until my lips meet his in a lazy, tired kiss.

I collapse onto the bed next to him. We're both sweaty and exhausted, but I've never been quite this elated in my life.

"That was amazing," I whisper, moving to untie his hands.

Oliver turns his head to look at me. "Princess, amazing doesn't even begin to describe what that was. Holy fuck."

"I'm glad you liked it as much as I did." I toss the rope onto the far side of the bed. When he doesn't move to touch me, I swallow hard. "Can you . . . um. Can you hold me?"

"Yes. God, of course, Wren." Instantly, his hands are on me. He rolls onto his side and pulls me into his body, cocooning me with his arms. "Are you okay?"

"I am," I whisper. "I'm more than okay."

He holds me silently, kissing the top of my head. We stay so still for long enough that we both drift off into a light sleep. I don't wake until I feel him shift against me, raising his head to look at the clock on his nightstand.

"We should probably get up," he says. "It's been twenty minutes."

Groaning, I force myself into a sitting position. Lying there with Oliver was so nice. The last thing I want to do is leave the warmth of his arms.

"We can shower separately," Oliver says, stretching his arms with a yawn. "You can go first if you'd like."

"I think I can handle us taking one together." I start to lift my nightgown up.

Oliver grabs my wrists, making sure to keep his grip gentle. "No, princess. I don't want you to just be able to handle it. Wait until you're one hundred percent ready."

"I am. I promise."

He pulls my hands away from my body, forcing me to let go of my nightgown. "You don't need to push yourself so hard."

"I'm not!"

The look he gives me says he doesn't believe me. Not even a little.

I sigh. "I can't say I'll feel the same way tomorrow. Or the day after that. But right now, I'm good. I want this."

For a second, he watches me with his eyes narrowed. But then he nods. "Okay. I'll get the water warming up."

I follow him into the bathroom. Maybe he's right to be concerned about me pushing myself too fast, but at least in this moment, I feel fine. I feel strong. Supported.

Oliver doesn't watch while I strip, which I appreciate. I'm fine, but it still makes me feel cared for. Only after I've stepped into the stream of water with him does he finally look at me.

"Still good?" he asks, and I catch a hint of nervousness in his tone.

"Still good," I say, kissing him lightly. "Can I wash you?"

He smiles. "Sure."

Oliver stands still while I soap him up and scrub his skin with a washcloth. When I accidentally go too lightly on his sides, he laughs and squirms, grabbing my wrists.

"Oops, sorry."

He raises an eyebrow. "Rhett's told me and Ell about your love for tickling him. You're not fooling me."

"It was an accident," I insist, but then I burst into an involuntary fit of giggles. I truly *wasn't* doing it on purpose, but now he'll never believe me.

He takes the washcloth from me with a playfully cautious glare. "I'd like to get through this shower without slipping and falling from your tickle attacks, thank you very much."

The mischievous sparkle in his eyes catches me off guard. There's always something so captivating about the way Oliver looks when he teases one of us. So I watch him while he runs the washcloth over his body.

He smirks. "I'd ask if you like what you see, but I already know the answer."

I smile shyly. Never in my life have I been so enraptured by a man performing such a simple task. But, I suppose, I've never felt this way about a person before, either. Or had someone feel this way about me.

You're my favorite part of Fridays.

I'd die a thousand deaths if it meant you got out of here alive.

I think I've made it pretty clear that whenever you're concerned, careful flies right out the window.

"Oliver," I whisper.

"Hmm?"

"I love you, too."

He freezes, his washcloth right over the butterfly tattoo on his chest. For a moment I'm afraid I said the wrong thing, or the right thing too late. I open my mouth, but I don't know how to make it right.

"Fuck." Oliver throws his washcloth to the floor. Then he places his hands on my hips and backs me into the shower wall. The tiles are freezing against my skin, but his arms encircle my waist, pressing me into his warmth.

When Oliver fits his mouth to mine, my body sags in relief. He keeps the kiss slow and languid, exploratory yet worshipful. As our tongues meet, gently sliding against each other, I wonder if he was worried I didn't say it back until now. I hope not. I'm glad he had the courage to say it first.

One of his hands leaves my waist, coming up to hold my head. "I was so scared I said it too early," he whispers against my lips. "The logical side of me knows it's too fast. But the rest of me knows how real this feels. How fucking *right* it is. You belong with us, Wren. There's nothing that could change my mind. Every time I look at you, it just solidifies it more in my head. I'm never letting you go. I could never want to."

I kiss him again, laughing as I do. Well, it's a half-laugh, half-sob. There are no tears in my eyes, but my heart feels so full I'm afraid it'll burst.

"I'm not letting you go either, O," I say when we pull away. "Ever. And I'll always remember. I'll always remember that you came for me the second you could."

He leans his forehead against mine, breathing hard. "I'd do it again in a heartbeat. There isn't a single thing I wouldn't do for you."

"I know," I whisper, pressing my lips to his again.

We finish showering. The whole time, Oliver can't help smiling, even when he shuts off the water and we have to step into the cold. He grabs a towel, but I take it from him and dry him off myself.

"You three always take care of me," I say. "I want to take care of you, too."

That just makes his smile widen.

By the time I've finished drying us both off, my mind is already whirring. Since they saved me, the guys have done nothing but remind me they're here for me in every sense of the phrase. They've spent god knows how much money on me, they've fussed over me every second of every day, and they've made sure every need I have gets met immediately.

There isn't anything else I could ask for. They're entirely committed to me. And it's exactly what I need to finish this.

As we're getting dressed, I say, "I think tomorrow is the day."

"For . . . ?" Oliver asks. But his smile is gone, and the look on his face tells me he already knows exactly what I mean.

I take a shaky breath. Then I square my shoulders and look him in the eye. "To kill Jordan."

CHAPTER TWENTY

Rhett

Oliver seems happier. No, not seems. *Is*. I think I know why, but I don't ask. That's between him and Wren. All I care about is that I get to see him smile more.

Obviously the kidnapping traumatized Wren the most, but I'm not stupid enough to believe Oliver isn't dealing with the aftereffects as well. He had to watch her almost die while he was tied to a chair, completely helpless. Hell, it's possible he almost died himself.

He's a master at redirecting conversations away from himself or hiding behind jokes, but Ell and I know better. We all need to heal from this, but Oliver and Wren do the most.

Still, his footsteps are lighter, and his eyes have gained back the sparkle that Wren's haven't. It's an odd cocktail of feelings, being relieved for Oliver yet concerned for Wren. But I'm not sure how to help her.

Until Thursday morning, that is. We're all in the kitchen eating breakfast, and Wren is staring into her coffee. Our doctor came and checked on her yesterday, saying she was much better, so she practically demanded coffee this morning.

Oliver nudges her with his elbow. "Tell them what you told me yesterday, princess."

She looks up, first making eye contact with me and then Elliot. "I want to kill Jordan today."

I didn't realize how tense I was until my whole body sags. I lean against the counter to disguise the movement, but I think Wren is the only one who falls for it.

I wanted to give her the time and space she needed, but I've hated having Jordan here. Every time I remember he's locked up in that room, I have to stop myself from storming in there and beating him to within an inch of his life.

"We can get everything set up," Elliot says. "There's actually an old clawfoot tub in the basement. It's chipped on one side. A little sharp, so we'll have to avoid that spot. But we can fill it with water."

She nods slowly. Her eyes flit to mine again. "You're still . . . ?"

"Absolutely, sweetheart."

With a relieved sigh, she takes a sip of her coffee. "I want to talk to him beforehand. Alone."

"No," all three of us say at the same time.

"Jesus," she mutters.

"That's a horrible idea, princess."

"Fine. With Rhett, then?" She gives me a questioning look.

I nod.

"When?" Elliot asks.

"After breakfast?"

"We can make that work."

It doesn't take us long to finish eating and clean up. Then Oliver and Elliot head to the basement. Wren takes my hand, and we walk toward Jordan's room silently.

Once we reach the door, Wren stops. I'm not sure what she wants to say to him, but she seems determined to have this conversation. Just as I'm about to remind her she doesn't have to do anything she doesn't want to, she takes a deep breath and unlocks the door.

Inside, Jordan is awake and seething. "What, no breakfast today?" he spits out. When neither of us answer, the resentment on his face morphs into realization. "No."

"You knew this was coming," Wren says.

"I didn't think you'd follow through!" Jordan shakes his head. "No, you don't have to do this. I was just avenging my brother. You understand that."

"If you wanted revenge, then you shouldn't've gone after an innocent person," I snap. Wren grabs my arm, and I realize I'm halfway to the bed, my fists clenched. I step back. "And you should've gone after the person who ordered the kill, not the people who fulfilled it."

Jordan ignores me, looking Wren up and down. "This is what you want? You can't wash this kind of blood off your hands. I hope you've thought long and hard about whether you really want to take my life."

I'm about to spit out a retort when Wren holds up her hand. It's hard to stay quiet, but this is for her, not me.

"How much thought did you put into killing me?" Wren asks, walking right up to him.

Jordan clamps his mouth shut.

"None, right?" Wren says, crossing her arms over her chest. "I was just a means to an end for you. A way to inflict pain on them." She gestures to me. "You didn't care that I didn't deserve it."

He refuses to look at her, staring straight ahead. Fucking coward.

God, I can't wait to kill him.

"I want you to know," Wren says, "that even though I won't be the one to kill you, it was my decision. I say when you die, not them. I'm sorry you lost your brother. Truly, I am. But it doesn't redeem what you did."

For a second, I'm afraid Jordan will try to latch onto the scrap of compassion Wren offered him. But he glances at me, and my expression must make him think better of it. So instead, he accepts his fate.

"I don't regret it," he says. "I may not have been able to execute all of you, but I had all three of your men scrambling to get to you like scared puppy dogs. I got to see the downright terror in Oliver's eyes while I drowned you. He was so desperate, he begged—"

Wren slaps him across the face, which takes me by surprise. "Say Oliver's name again, and I will put you through so much pain that you'll be begging god to erase you from all of existence."

I can't help the smile that spreads over my face.

Protective rage looks good on you, sweetheart.

"Fuck you," Jordan seethes.

Ignoring him, Wren turns to me. "I'm ready."

I untie Jordan from the bed. His wrists are still bound, so I yank him to his feet. The idiot tries to get away, but it's barely an inconvenience for me. I keep a firm grip on him as we head to the basement. The stairs are a little tricky, but I make Jordan go first so he has no choice but to descend.

Oliver and Elliot have dragged the tub into the middle of the floor and filled it to the brim with water. When Jordan sees it, he starts struggling again, but it's in vain. I force him forward until he's standing in front of the tub. Then I look to Wren for instruction.

She moves to stand in between Oliver and Elliot. "Get him on his knees."

I push Jordan to the ground in front of the tub. He tries to get back up, but I don't let him.

Wren continues hovering a couple yards away. I'm not sure why she doesn't want to get up close for this, but I suppose it's a lot for her. Jordan may have almost killed her half a dozen times, but this is still quite an adjustment to the life Wren was living a month ago.

"Put him under," she whispers.

I oblige, grabbing the hair at the base of Jordan's neck and shoving his face into the water. He thrashes, trying to get free, but I cage his body to the tub in the same way he did to Wren.

When Jordan's movements slow, Wren says, "Up."

Once I've pulled him out of the water, Jordan sputters and coughs. "Fuck you," he growls once he's gotten enough air.

"Maybe you should stop struggling," Wren says dryly. "You're making it harder on yourself."

"You bit-"

I don't wait for Wren's permission this time, forcing Jordan underwater before he can finish his sentence. She watches with a hardened gaze, lifting her chin after a few seconds.

When I pull Jordan out of the water, he's shaking.

"Please," he gasps. "I'll leave you alone. I'll give you whatever you want. Money, my inheritance, anything. Please just give me a second chance."

Wren is silent for a moment, and I begin to worry she's actually considering Jordan's offer. But then she asks quietly, "Were you going to give me a second chance?"

He doesn't answer.

"Were you?" she shouts.

Jordan cringes and shakes his head.

"Then you don't get one. Rhett." She points to the tub.

When I push Jordan down this time, he doesn't fight. I keep my eyes on Wren, waiting for her to tell me to pull him up, but she doesn't. She's frozen, holding onto one of Elliot's hands and one of Oliver's.

"Sweetheart?" I say.

"Keep him down."

Eventually, Jordan's body sags against the tub. He's unconscious, but he's still not dead. I look to Wren, but she doesn't give me any indication that she wants me to move him yet.

"How long . . . how long does it take?" she asks after a couple minutes.

"He's not coming back from this, princess," Oliver says.

With a shuddering breath, she says, "Let him go."

I pull Jordan out and lay him on the floor. Then I check for his pulse. Non-existent.

"He's dead, sweetheart."

Wren stares at Jordan's body, almost as if she's waiting for him to reanimate or something. But then her gaze moves to me. She steps forward, but then she pauses. "Come here. Please."

I do, searching her face for any hint of regret. But all I find is a trust so deep it could rival the ocean.

Grabbing my head, Wren pulls me down and slams her lips to mine. I don't miss a beat, gripping her waist and matching the intensity of her kiss. I use so much force I'm afraid I'm hurting her, but she doesn't back down. And then she's practically crawling onto me, and I'm picking her up so she can lock her legs around my torso.

She pulls away to catch her breath, but it's only a second before she descends on me again. Her tongue enters my mouth in a gentle caress before I practically shove mine down her throat.

When we break off the kiss, my chest is heaving. I stare into her eyes, and there—I can just make out a sliver of brightness shining in them, resurrected because Jordan is dead.

Fuck. I'll kill every person who's ever hurt her if it means I get to see her full of happiness and life again.

"I want you," she breathes. "All three of you."

"You have us, sweetheart."

She shakes her head. "At once. Now."

I glance at Elliot and Oliver, who look equally relieved and concerned. "You're sure, sweetheart?"

Resting her forehead against mine, she says, "I've never been so sure of something in my life."

CHAPTER TWENTY-ONE

Elliot

We leave Jordan's body in the basement to deal with later. As we head upstairs, my phone buzzes in my pocket, so I pull it out. My heart is instantly in my throat when I see who's calling.

"I'll catch up with you guys in a minute," I say.

"Suit yourself," Oliver says.

I watch them go, waiting until I'm out of earshot to answer my phone. "Ludo. What can I do for you?"

"Always getting straight to the point," he says. "It's one of the many things I admire about you."

I roll my eyes. That's the nice thing about talking on the phone with Ludo. When it comes to my facial expressions, I don't have to pretend I don't loathe the man.

"I'm going on vacation to Florida next week," Ludo continues. "I'm bringing my fiancée with me, and unfortunately I have to attend to some business while I'm down there. My bodyguards will be with me, so I need someone to watch over her. And considering how brilliantly you three handled Edgar Williams, I thought I'd extend the job offer to you first."

"Thank you for the opportunity," I say on autopilot.

Next week. Florida. Shit.

This is the perfect chance to get closer to Ludo and maybe even gain some more personal information on him. If we're going to be spending a significant amount of time with his fiancée, then we can probably get her to open up.

The only problem is that we told Wren we wouldn't leave her here alone again. This is a no-brainer opportunity for us, but I refuse to go back on our promise. We could bring her with us, but there's no way she'll be comfortable with that.

Fuck. What if she says no?

What if she says yes? How do we keep her safe while we're working?

"When do you need an answer by?" I ask.

"Tomorrow afternoon, preferably."

"I'll talk to the others."

I don't bother saying goodbye, ending the call and rushing to catch up with the others. Right now, the only thing I care about is the three of them. Ludo can wait.

In Rhett's room, I find Oliver sitting on the bed with Wren in his lap. He's kissing her softly, and she's holding onto him so tightly I wonder if it hurts. Out of all of us, these two are the most openly affectionate—probably because they're the ones who need affection the most. Seeing them give it to each other so freely warms my heart.

I can hear water running in the bathroom, so Rhett must be taking a shower. Understandable. I'd want to wash Jordan off of me, too.

Wren pulls away from Oliver and immediately spots me. Then she smiles. "You look happy, Ell."

"I am."

Gently, I lower myself onto the bed next to them. When Oliver cranes his neck toward me, I brush my fingers along his jaw before kissing him. Then I kiss Wren, wrapping one arm around her and my other around

Oliver. When we pull away, my heart is so full I can't help the huge grin that takes over my face. Now all I need is for Rhett to get his ass out of the shower so I can have all three of them in my arms.

"Who was on the phone?" Oliver asks.

"We'll talk about it later." I kiss him again, harder than before.

Since we got Oliver and Wren back, I haven't been able to get enough of him. I was terrified I'd never see him again, that he'd die before I got another chance to hold him or kiss him or see his eyes light up when he laughs. So I've kept him as close as I can. I've had to share him with Rhett and Wren, but I've hogged him a little. *I was just so damn scared.*

"Hey. Ell, hey. We're okay." Wren strokes her hand down my back soothingly.

When I pull away, I realize I'm shaking. "Fuck. I'm never letting you two out of my sight again."

Oliver laughs. "That might be a little inconvenient."

"I don't care," I say firmly. And then I kiss him again, gripping the back of his shirt. After a minute, I move to Wren, pausing for a second at the soft concern in her eyes. I do my best to kiss it right out of her. They both have entirely too much anxiety to be worried about me.

I'll be okay. As long as I don't lose any of you.

When we break off our kiss, we realize Rhett is standing in the bathroom doorway with only a towel wrapped around his waist. All three of us stare at him for a second too long, and he smirks.

"C'mere," Wren says, reaching out to him.

He sits on the other side of her and Oliver, wrapping his arms around them like I am. Wren ends up cocooned between the three of us, and she sighs contentedly, relaxing into our embrace.

"Thank you," she whispers. "For everything. For saving me, for taking care of me, for being so understanding." She shifts in Oliver's lap so she can look at Rhett. "And for killing him. For killing all of them."

Rhett tightens his arms around her and Oliver, leaning down and kissing her at the same time. "I'd do it again." He leaves a kiss on her jawbone. "And again." Another on her neck. "And again." Then her shoulder. "As many times as it takes, sweetheart."

Tears spring into her eyes, but she blinks them back. "I know."

We all hold each other tightly. It's been multiple days since we brought Wren and Oliver home, but now that we've dealt with Jordan, I feel like I can finally relax. I know Rhett feels the same way, and I wouldn't be surprised if Oliver and Wren do, as well.

Speaking of Wren, she seems more relaxed than I expected. She said she wants all of us, but it was in the heat of the moment. If she wants to back out, I want to make sure she knows we won't get upset.

"Ell, I'm fine," she says, and it takes me a second to realize my thoughts must be written on my face. "I trust you. All of you. There's no reason for me to be scared." She turns to look at Oliver, her gaze softening. "No reason at all," she murmurs, running her fingers over his lips.

"Kiss me, princess," Oliver whispers.

She does, grabbing onto his hair. He grips her waist, groaning into her mouth and letting her maneuver his head to the angle she wants. When she releases him, her eyes are unfocused, glazed over with want and need.

"Now you two kiss," Wren says, glancing between me and Rhett.

The last thing I'd ever do is deny these three anything. So when Rhett grabs the back of my neck and yanks me toward him, I kiss him with the same ferocity that's burning in his eyes. He bites my lip so hard I taste blood, so I do the same to him, releasing Wren and Oliver and grabbing his shoulders. When I dig my fingers into his skin, he lets out a grunt of pleasure.

"Holy shit," Wren whispers.

"So fucking hot," Oliver mutters.

I turn my head and smirk at him. "Jealous?"

"Nah. I know you can't stay away from me."

"Damn right I can't." I stand, picking Wren up and setting her in Rhett's lap. Then I shove Oliver onto his back and crawl on top of him. I give myself a split second to absorb the grin on his face before I fuse my mouth to his.

Oliver practically blooms under my touch, the way he always does when I kiss him. He latches onto my arms and follows my lead as I take the kiss from heated and passionate to slow and meaningful. By the time I'm finished with him, his dick is hard against me, and I'm so turned on my cock is pressing painfully against my jeans.

"These," I say as I get up and reach for Oliver's pants, "are coming off. Now."

He undoes my button and zipper, trying to pull my pants down as I try to get his. I have to swat his hands away and do it myself because he was just getting in the way. I make sure to yank his boxers down too, and he tears off his shirt eagerly.

Then we both hear Wren moan. She's straddling Rhett, and he has her shirt and bra pushed up to her neck. He's leaning her back slightly, keeping a firm grip on her shoulders while he sucks on one of her nipples.

Oliver sits up. "Bring her over here."

Rhett doesn't acknowledge him at first, either because he wants to keep Wren to himself or because he got so caught up in the moment that it took a second for Oliver's words to register. But then Rhett stands, lifting Wren and turning around.

Wren laughs when he throws her onto the bed next to Oliver. He leans over her, running his fingers along the waistband of her pants.

"Can I take them off, sweetheart?"

She nods, lifting her ass when he pulls them down her legs. Then she pulls her shirt and bra over her head, tossing them to the floor.

None of us move. This is the farthest any of us have gone with her since the kidnapping. She told me the other day that even when she was with Oliver, she kept some lingerie on.

"I'm okay," she whispers, propping herself up on her elbows. "Please touch me."

I still hesitate. There's no way she bounced back this quickly. And maybe she's okay right now, but overall? There are going to be a lot of ups and downs.

Oliver moves first, rolling onto his side and curling an arm around her stomach. He leaves a trail of kisses from her shoulder to her fingertips, causing her to shiver at the light touch.

Rhett touches her next, lying next to her and pulling a moan from her lips when he kisses her. I move in between her legs and drag my mouth up her thigh. When I reach her panties, I press a kiss to the fabric. Then I lightly tickle her through them, making her moan again.

"Please," she begs me.

Tugging her panties to the side, I swipe my tongue from her entrance to her clit. She gasps into Rhett's mouth. I do it again at the same time Oliver runs his tongue over one of her nipples, eliciting a similar reaction from her.

Perfect.

I suck on her clit gently for a few minutes, but I want a different angle. "Get up," I say, tapping her thigh.

She does, and I flip over onto my back. Rhett smirks at me, knowing exactly what I want. So he helps Wren get into position until she's facing him and hovering right over my face. I grip her thighs and pull her down, circling her clit with my tongue.

Crying out, she grabs Rhett's arms. He kisses her, capturing her moans in his mouth. And then, in true Rhett fashion, he wraps one of his hands around Wren's throat.

"Don't squeeze," she whispers. "Please don't squeeze. I need to be able to breathe."

"I know," he says quietly, stroking her hair with his free hand. He brushes his nose against hers. "I won't."

The bed shifts as Oliver crawls out of my limited view. I don't think much of it until I feel him running his tongue up the length of my cock.

"Fuck," I groan against Wren, making her whimper.

As Oliver takes my dick into his mouth, I do my best to focus on Wren. I alternate between stroking her clit with my tongue and sucking on it, letting her reactions guide me. I may have learned a lot about what she likes over the past weeks, but I'm no fool. There's still plenty of Wren's body for me to explore.

Oliver, on the other hand, has had ten years to explore *mine,* and he's too fucking good at blow jobs. With one hand gripping the base, he focuses on the head of my cock, sucking and using his tongue to tease me.

"Don't make me come, dammit," I growl.

I hear—and feel—him chuckle.

Fuck.

"Ell," Wren moans. She's still caught in Rhett's embrace, stroking his dick clumsily from the awkward angle. Or maybe it's because she's having trouble focusing.

I squeeze her legs, sucking on her clit to bring all of her attention back to me. It only takes a few minutes before she's lost the ability to form a complete sentence. Rhett keeps his hand on her throat and his eyes locked with hers as she gets closer and closer to falling apart.

When I feel myself approaching the edge, I pull away for a split second. *"Oliver."*

He gives me one last, long suck that almost makes me lose it on the spot. *Holy shit.* But I'm already focusing on Wren again. I want to keep her on the brink of her orgasm for as long as I can, but I don't. There will be other times for building the tension in her body to an unbearable point. But today is about worshiping her and reminding her she's safe with us.

And making her come so many times she can't stand, of course.

It only takes another minute or two before Wren's legs are tightening around my head. I go the tiniest bit faster, pulling a guttural moan from her throat. Then she tenses and cries out.

"Oh no, oh god. Ell, I can't . . . no, *fuck.*"

At first I wonder why she said no, and I'm about to stop, but then it hits me—literally. Keeping a firm grip on her thighs, I lap up every drop as Wren squirts almost directly into my mouth.

"Just let go, sweetheart," Rhett says.

She moans my name into Rhett's chest as I lick her gently. Only once she's fully come down from her high do I stop. I press one more kiss to her clit, making her hips jerk, before I crawl out from underneath her. By the time I'm sitting up, she still has her face buried against Rhett's chest.

"Love?"

She lets out a muffled sound.

"Sweetheart," Rhett says, drawing back a couple inches. He removes his hand from her throat, cups her chin, and smiles down at her. "It's okay."

She shakes her head. "I've never done that with another person before. Definitely not on someone's *face*. Ell, I—"

"Don't you dare apologize," I say firmly. "It's a part of sex, love. And it was fucking hot."

She grimaces, but Rhett kisses her gently, still holding her chin. Oliver comes up beside me, pressing his lips to my shoulder. I grab him and shove him onto his back.

"You and your devilish tongue."

He grins up at me. "You love it."

I groan. "More than you know."

I kiss the life out of him, our tongues tangling in a dance for control. *Fuck,* I want him so bad. But not right now.

"You're sleeping with me tonight," I say lowly in his ear, "so I can fuck you in the morning."

"Oh, I'll never say no to that." He kisses me once more before I get off of him. "Princess, I want to eat you out while Elliot fucks you."

"H . . . how?" she says, scrunching up her face while she tries to think through the logistics.

Fucking adorable.

"Oh, there are a few ways," Oliver replies with a wink.

I come up behind her and stroke her arms. As I nuzzle my face into her neck, she relaxes into me, giving Rhett another kiss before he gets out of Oliver's way.

"Wanna join?" I ask.

"Oh, I'm perfectly happy watching." Rhett's heated gaze rakes over the three of us as he settles against the headboard. "For now."

I press Wren's back to my front, running my lips up her neck before nibbling on her earlobe. My cock rubs in between her legs, and she whines, trying to grind against it.

It takes me a second to get the angle right, and then I slide into her. I loop my arms through hers to keep her against me, thrusting into her gently.

Fuck. It's barely been a week since I've been inside her, but it feels like it's been ten years. I groan into her neck as she clenches around my dick.

"Ahhh, oh my god, Elliot."

"It's Ell, love. You call me Ell now," I say, thrusting into her harder.

"*Ell,*" she cries.

"That's my girl," I murmur.

The bed shifts as Oliver crawls in front of her. I can't see what he's doing, but based on the way Wren moans and clamps down on me, it's exactly what he said he would.

"Oh, fuck," she pants.

God, I love it when she's like this.

It doesn't take long before Wren comes. Neither Oliver nor I stop, forcing her higher until she's screaming and convulsing against me. When I finally slow, she goes limp in my arms with a moan.

Oliver scrambles to his knees, cupping her face and kissing her. "I love the way you sound when you come, princess."

"I love *you,*" she whispers.

I pause, glancing at Rhett. We were wondering if Oliver told her what he told me, and if she said it back. I guess this is our confirmation.

"I love you too, Wren," Oliver says with a smile. Then he trails a hand down her body, reaching in between her legs. "Help me make her come again, Ell."

Tightening my grip on Wren's arms, I slide in and out of her, keeping my pace slow. I'm too close to last long, so Oliver is going to have to get her going first.

"Fuck," Wren moans. She leans her head back on my shoulder.

"You're doing so well," I murmur when she starts to tremble. I go harder, groaning when she clamps down on my dick. "God, you're going to make me come if you keep doing that."

"Ell," she sobs.

"Oh fuck yes," Oliver says, moving his hand faster. "That's it, princess. Give it to us."

It takes a few more seconds, but then she explodes, coming all over my dick with a loud groan. With every orgasm, it feels like she's surrendering herself over to us more and more. She's letting go of everything holding her back and falling into us with complete abandon.

We've got you, love. We'll catch you.

Oliver slams his lips to Wren's as she reaches the peak of her orgasm. The way she melts into him, opening her mouth so he can slip his tongue inside, is too hot of an image for me to handle. I come with one last thrust and a breathless moan.

"That's what I figured would happen," Oliver says with a smirk. Then he grabs the hair at the base of my neck, angling my head so he can fuse his mouth to mine. He controls the kiss, and I let him, too tired and sated to fight.

When I open my eyes, it's to Rhett crawling over and tugging Wren from in between me and Oliver. He has her lie on her back, moving in between her legs. Wren's expression softens as she gazes up at him.

"Is this okay?" he asks. "Like this?"

She nods, opening her legs more for him. He notches his dick at her entrance, groaning as he does. And then he leans down, propping himself up on his elbows while cradling her head with both hands. I don't think I've ever seen Rhett handle something—or someone—so delicately.

"Sweetheart," he murmurs, sliding deep into her.

She moans, arching into him. "Rhett. Rhett, please kiss me. Please—"

He captures the rest of her words with his lips on hers. The kiss immediately deepens as he slowly pulls out and slides into her again. She locks her legs around his waist, keeping him close to her.

"Call me your beautiful whore," she whispers. "Plea-"

He kisses her again. "No begging. Today, we'll give you whatever you ask for." Then he leans down, placing his lips right by her ear and whispering. Just then, he picks up the pace of his thrusts.

Wren cries out, clinging to his shoulders. "Rhett, oh fuck."

He groans. "Say my name again."

"Rhett," she whispers. She moves her hips to meet his thrusts, whimpering.

"You want more?"

"I want two of you inside of me," she pants.

"DP?"

She shakes her head, snaking one of her hands down and sliding two fingers inside of her with Rhett's cock. It pulls a moan from both of them. "Here. Like Ell said the other day."

"Fuck," Oliver mutters. I've been stroking his cock slowly, but I don't think he has that reaction because of me.

"You want to fuck her with him inside of her?" I say.

"God. Yes."

"O, get over here," Rhett says gruffly. "And bring the lube."

He grabs it while Rhett and Wren readjust so he's lying on his back and she's on top of him. She waits until Rhett has spread some lube over his cock before lowering herself onto him.

"Lean forward, sweetheart."

She does, placing her hands on Rhett's shoulders for balance. Oliver inserts two fingers into her, rubbing against Rhett's dick. Slowly, Wren moves up and down to get used to the feeling.

"Just like that, princess," Oliver says. "We're going to take our time getting you ready."

They do, adding one finger at a time and making sure Wren isn't too uncomfortable. By the time they're done, she's squirming impatiently.

"C'mere, sweetheart," Rhett says, tugging her down and kissing her. "Give Oliver some room."

Oliver settles behind Wren, squeezing her ass. "You ready, princess?"

"Yes," Wren whispers. "I want you to both come inside of me."

Groaning at the thought, Oliver lines himself up. Slowly, he slides in with Rhett's cock, stretching her. "Christ, Wren."

She whimpers, digging her nails into Rhett's arms.

"Tell us if it hurts, sweetheart."

"No, it's good. Please don't stop."

Oliver keeps his hands on Wren's hips to hold her steady, pulling out and then sliding back in. All three of them groan.

I smile, my gaze fixated on the spot where they're both stretching her wide open. "You're taking them so beautifully, love."

By this point, Wren is so overstimulated she's barely with us. I'm not surprised when she comes first, or when she pulls Rhett with her.

"Fuck." Oliver stares down at them, breathing hard. *"Fuck."*

"I know," Rhett says. He's stroking Wren's hair while she has her face buried in his neck.

"Rhett," Oliver groans. He keeps his gaze locked with Rhett's as he finishes. When he pulls out, their cum leaks out of Wren.

"So fucking hot," I mutter.

As Rhett eases out of Wren, Oliver leans down and kisses her back. "How did that feel, princess?"

"I want to do it again," she pants. "Oh god, not now. Some other time. I want Oliver and Ell. And then I want Ell and Rhett."

I smile, helping her off of Rhett and pulling her into my lap. "There's nothing I'd like more."

We catch our breath for a few minutes, but we're all sweaty and a little sticky.

"Come shower with me, love," I say, helping Wren to her feet.

"You come right back here when you're done," Oliver says. "I have questions." He gives me a pointed look.

Odd.

In my room, I get the shower turned on and pull Wren under the water. She's shivering already since she isn't pressed up against one of us anymore.

"How are you feeling?" I ask.

She nods, hugging herself, which isn't the response I was looking for.

"Hey. Is this okay? Do you need me to step out while you finish?"

"What? No, you're fine. I was just thinking. I . . . I don't want to take a bath today."

"Oh. That's fine, love."

I always enjoy soaking in the bath with Wren, and I'll miss the time with her. But as long as she doesn't think she'll be too sore without it, I don't mind. It's not like we'll never do it again.

Gently, I scrub her down, and she insists on doing the same to me. I used to think it was weird—the idea of your partner washing you. But then Rhett started doing it, and I realized it's one of the ways he tells me he loves me since he has so much trouble saying the words. Ever since then, I've always looked forward to it.

Out of the shower, we dry off and get changed quickly. I'm curious what Oliver has questions about. By the time we make it back to Rhett's room, they're already changing the sheets.

"So," Oliver says. "Who called you?" One of his eyebrows is raised in what almost looks like a challenge, and I realize he already knows.

"You heard."

He nods.

"I didn't," Wren says.

Oliver grins. "You were too busy kissing Rhett all over his neck while he carried you down the hallway."

Grabbing one of the blankets that fell off the bed, I drape it over Wren's shoulders. This conversation has the potential to send her mind to dark places, so I keep an arm around her.

"It was Ludo," I say.

Rhett freezes. "What did he want?"

"He offered us a job. Not the usual kind, though. He needs a bodyguard for his fiancée while they're on a trip next week."

"Next week?" Oliver exclaims. "Jesus. That's short notice."

I nod in agreement. "From what he said, it sounds to me like he had some last-minute business to deal with, and he's turning it into a vacation. God knows why."

When I look to Wren, she has the blanket pulled tight around her. *Fuck.* I was hoping she wouldn't immediately get nervous.

"What I said still stands, love. We're not leaving you behind. So if you say yes to this—and that's *if* you say yes, because you don't have to—then we're taking you with us."

She nods slowly, staring at the bed. "This would help you guys? With your revenge plans?"

"Yes," Rhett says. He's gripping a pillow tightly, and his jaw is clenched.

Please don't pressure her. Please don't—

"Can I think about it?" she asks, her voice small and quiet.

"Of course, sweetheart," Rhett says. I have no idea how he's so tense yet manages to speak so gently to her. "Ell, when do we need an answer by?"

"Tomorrow afternoon."

"I'll have an answer by tonight," she says.

Rhett sighs. Then he tosses his pillow onto the bed. "I need to sleep."

Good. He's so behind on rest, I don't know how he's functioning.

Wren fidgets with her blanket. "Can I stay with you?"

"Sure."

"Make sure he doesn't get on his phone," Oliver says to Wren. "He says it helps him relax, but he always ends up on news sites. And that's stressful as hell."

Rhett grumbles something under his breath while Oliver kisses his cheek and then Wren's. I have to hide my smile as I take Wren into my arms, pressing my lips to the top of her head. Then I kiss Rhett softly, wishing I could reach inside of him and take some of the dark thoughts swirling in his mind.

Grabbing Oliver's hand, I lead him out of the room. "Sleep well, you two."

Chapter Twenty-Two

Wren

Waking up in Rhett's arms is one of my favorite feelings.

It's not that I don't love waking up with Elliot and Oliver. I love it just as much. But since Rhett's sleep schedule is so different, I don't get to do it nearly as often with him. Plus there's something about the way he holds me that fills my heart to the brim.

Carefully, I roll over so I'm facing him. My hope is not to wake him, but when I turn, he's already wide awake.

I frown. "Did you not sleep?"

"I did." He kisses my forehead. "Woke up an hour ago."

"And you just . . . stayed?"

He swallows, and his gaze flicks away. "Didn't want to let you go."

Butterflies take flight in my stomach. Nuzzling my face against his chest, I say, "I like that."

"What?"

"You not letting me go."

He hums lowly, tightening his arms around me. I don't miss the tension riddling his muscles, but hopefully I'll be able to ease some of his stress soon.

I've made up my mind. If I'm being honest, I made my decision the second Elliot explained the situation. I just wanted a little time to sit with it before I jumped into something that'll probably scare the shit out of me.

Ever since I cut off Thomas and distanced myself from my mom, I've been going through the process of healing from the damage they caused me. And ever since I was taken Friday night, the amount of things I need to heal from and work through has only grown.

The guys have been nothing but supportive of me. They've done their best to be what I need exactly when I need it. It makes me feel so treasured it hurts. Even more than that, it makes me want them to know I care about them just as much.

Seeing how much pain Rhett is in whenever Sammy is mentioned makes my heart ache. And as I was falling asleep, I realized something. Getting revenge on Ludo is part of *his* healing process. And I refuse to stand in the way of that.

"We should talk," I say quietly. "All four of us."

Rhett goes so stiff I have to poke him to make sure he didn't actually turn to stone.

"Breathe," I whisper. "Nothing's wrong."

Grudgingly, he inhales deeply. "Can we find them now?"

"Of course." I start to move, but then I hit an obstacle. "Um. Rhett."

"Hmm?"

"You have to let go of me."

He frowns, looking down to where my body is pressed to his. "No."

It's awkward, but he gets the blankets off of us and keeps me in his arms while he gets up. In the bathroom, he sets me on the counter, staying in between my legs while we brush our teeth. And when it's time to go downstairs, I reach up to him. He picks me up again, hugging me tightly and carrying me.

I wrap my legs around his torso and bury my face in his neck. For a second, I'm worried I'm being too clingy, but then I think *fuck that*. Jordan stole me away from them. And even if he hadn't, I'm allowed to be as affectionate as I fucking want to. Rhett is dishing it out just as much as I am right now.

In the living room, we find Oliver on the couch with his head in Elliot's lap. Elliot is holding a book with one hand and has the other resting on Oliver's shoulder. They look relaxed. Happy. And the warm glow from the fireplace casts them in a cozy, romantic light.

"Have a good nap?" Elliot asks, looking up from his book.

The noise makes Oliver jump, and he lets out a tired groan.

"Oh, sorry." Elliot strokes his hair before bending down and kissing the top of his head. "I didn't realize you'd fallen asleep."

"Mmmph."

"Nap was fine," I say as Rhett sits in one of the armchairs, keeping an arm secured around my waist. "I want to talk."

Elliot sets his book on the end table, and Oliver pulls himself into a sitting position. They both watch me expectantly.

Clearing my throat, I shift in Rhett's lap, finding his hand and intertwining my fingers with his. "You three have done more for me than anyone ever has. You've shown me different perspectives on life. You've put yourselves in danger to keep me safe." I give Oliver a grateful look. "You've spent a *ridiculous* amount of money taking care of me."

"Not enough, if I have anything to say about it," Oliver mutters.

I giggle. But then my expression turns serious again. "Avenging Sammy is important to you three. It's important to me, too."

Rhett lets out an audible breath, his head falling back and hitting the cushion of the chair.

I turn so I can look at him. His gaze is as piercing as ever, yet there are no expectations in it. Just him. "What I'm trying to say is . . ."

Rhett's hand tightens on my waist, a flicker of hope sparking in his eyes.

I smile. "I'm in."

The story continues in Wretched Corruption.

DELETED SCENE

If you want to read one of the deleted scenes from Undying Resilience, go to subscribepage.io/ur-bonus and sign up to my email list.

Author's Note

Thanks so much for reading Undying Resilience! The Ruthless Desires characters have become some of my all-time favorites, and I love diving deeper into who they are. Their story continues in Wretched Corruption, which is book four out of six in the series.

I've been writing since I was a teenager. Creating different story-worlds and characters was my absolute favorite pastime (okay, okay, coping mechanism). I've always loved romance, especially dark romance with a little suspense sprinkled in, so it's no surprise it's what I ended up writing.

If you'd like to stay up to date with my latest writings and adventures, you can check out my website elirafirethorn.com or follow me on Instagram, Pinterest, and TikTok @elirafirethorn.

Also By Elira Firethorn

Dark Luxuries Trilogy

Deepest Obsession

Twisted Redemption

Darkest Retribution

Dark Luxuries Epilogue

Ruthless Desires Series

Blissful Masquerade

Perfect Convergence

Undying Resilience

Wretched Corruption

Standalones

Moonflower

Printed in Great Britain
by Amazon

35205285R00135